MW00939123

REVIEWS

D. Donovan, Senior Reviewer, Midwest Book Review

Robert M. Moores does a fine job of exploring Violet's many feelings. Young readers who turn to her story for insights about grief and family interactions will find The Shoebox creates a satisfying blend of mystery, intrigue, and psychological and spiritual revelations alike, connecting real-world events to religious and personal insights. The Shoebox is highly recommended for advanced elementary through middle school readers, who receive an inviting exploration of Violet's life and its many possibilities.

Debjeet Mukherjee-Readers' Favorite (5 star review)

Robert M. Moores has woven a wonderful tale that is heartwarming to read. It reassures our faith in God and teaches you some valuable lessons on life as a whole. The Shoe Box is a reassurance of the good in mankind, reiterating the fact that there are many good people in our lives who are willing to help us during times of despair. They act as messengers of God while we come to terms with what has happened and work towards rebuilding what is to come

G.M. Jakelic- Author of Aurora and God

I love the way this book is written. From the beginning, it takes you on a journey with a young girl, Violet.It is one of those books when you start reading, you won't put down until you finish it.It's a very captivating story and I love how violets emotions are so well described.I could also see this made as a movie! Recommended!

K.C. Finn- Readers Favorite (5 star review)

A touching drama that tackles its sensitive subject matter very well, this is a story in which a young girl deals with the tragedy and trauma of losing her father when she was four years old. Trapped between her past and her future, we follow Violet closely through her emotional journey to the discovery of the titular shoe box in the attic. Author Robert M. Moores has crafted a beautiful and emotionally intelligent work that deals with grief and loss in a caring fashion. One of the things which most impressed me about this story was its commitment to character and close narrative style, which not only gives us an accurate portrayal of the thoughts and feelings of the young heroine, but also a highly relatable account of how trauma and loss can haunt us from our youth.

Sherri Rosen (Award winning author/New York Times Bestseller list 63 weeks)

Robert Moores has written a delightful YA/fantasy book showing children that many times there are good reasons for some of the crazy up and down emotions they will have in their life,and how it's all okay,and there's a way out to gratitude, love, appreciation of friends and family. The story teaches the value of friendship, patience, love and understanding. The book made me feel that there's hope for the younger generation and that's something that's so important in this day and age.

THE SHOEBOX

The
Shoe Box

By Robert M. Moores

Palmetto Publishing Group
Charleston, SC

The Shoe BoxCopyright © 2020 by Robert M. Moores

All rights reserved

No portion of this book may be reproduced, stored in a retrieval system,
or transmitted in any form by any means—electronic, mechanical, photo-
copy, recording, or other—except for brief quotations in printed reviews,
without prior permission of the author.

First Edition

Printed in the United States

ISBN-13: 978-1-64990-134-7
ISBN-10: 1-64990-134-8
eBook ISBN: 978-1-64990-133-0

Prologue

On March 26, 2016, the Cooper family and their friends gathered to celebrate Violet Cooper's fourth birthday. The party featured pizza, a table full of desserts, a moon bounce, and a ton of games for the kids to play. Today was Violet's day, and her parents decided to go all out to show how much they loved their daughter. Violet was in the backyard playing with her cousins and friends while the adults were over at a table conversing among themselves. The kids brought out the water balloons and decided to have a good old fight. Violet's parents didn't really want her getting wet, but you only turn four once.

It was time to have cake and sing happy birthday to the birthday girl. Her mom and dad had gotten chocolate cake, which was Violet's favorite. Violet knew that she could get away with a little extra since it was her birthday, so she didn't wait for the cake to be cut. She took a handful of cake, stuffed her face, and got chocolate everywhere. On a normal day, her parents wouldn't have been too happy, but on her birthday, all they could do was laugh. Once everyone was done having cake, it would be time to open presents. Violet's mom insisted her daughter put new clothes on before this activity, so she took Violet to get changed.

As Violet was changing, her dad signaled for her mom to come over to him. Violet's mom told her to finish changing and let her know that she would be back. Her dad explained that he had to step out for a bit to get Violet's surprise present and would be back shortly. Violet saw that her dad was leaving, so when her mom came back, she asked where he was going.

"Where's Daddy going?"

"It's a surprise, and he'll be back in a little bit. Faster than you can say 'banana split,'" replied Violet's mom.

"Hey, that rhymed."

"How do you know what rhyming is?"

"Daddy reads me Dr. Seuss every night and explained rhyming to me."

"Let's head to the family room, where everyone is waiting to watch you open up the presents they got for you. Your dad will join us soon. Let's go."

One

It was a Tuesday morning, May 19, 2020, 7:10 a.m. in Orlando, Florida. Violet's alarm went off. It was time to get ready for school. Violet's head popped up from the pillow as she was startled, as usual, by the alarm. With displeasure she realized that it was time to get up but hit the snooze button and put her head back down. Every morning Violet's mom walked past her bedroom to see if she was up.

"Violet, you need to get up. You're going to be late."

"I know, Mother. Just give me a minute, and I'll be out of bed."

"Okay, sweetie. Hurry up! Your breakfast is going to get cold. I made your favorite! Also, I got a call from school last night, and we need to talk."

Five minutes later Violet rolled out of bed and headed to the bathroom to start getting ready. As she was about to walk out of the room, the calendar on her wall caught her eye. She noticed that it was the day she most dreaded: it was Father's Day as well as the daddy-daughter dance at her school, Founders Elementary. Violet hung her head in dismay as she walked to the bathroom. When she got to the bathroom, she stood in front of the mirror for quite some time, trying to convince herself that everything was going to be okay.

Violet thought to herself, *You're going to be all right. It's only one day out of the 365 days of the year. Then you have 364 days to prepare yourself all over again for this day.*

Violet hated Father's Day. Not only did it remind her more than any other day of the absence of her father, but it also reminded her that she never even got the chance to know him. She dreaded going to school today. Due to losing her dad four years earlier, she was going to miss out on the daddy-daughter dance and feel like the odd one out again. Violet then made up her mind that she was going to make the best of this day. She proceeded to get ready so she could be with her mom for breakfast and hear what she had to say.

"Hey, you made it," Violet's mom said. "Take a seat and enjoy. It's your favorite—waffles with strawberries and whip cream."

"I appreciate you doing this, Mom, but I'm not very hungry."

"Violet, you haven't been hungry the past few days, and now I'm getting calls from school that you haven't been yourself lately. You act this way around this time every year."

"That's easy for you to say; you've had your father around every Father's Day since you were a child."

"I know, honey, that this time of the year can be quite hard, but we have to be thankful for what God has given us."

"I'll be thankful when I have a dad again."

"Violet, we can talk about this later if you'd like. You know I'm always here. But, again, we have to make the best of what God has given us."

"I guess…"

"Let's get to the car, or you'll be late for school. Also, I want you to start seeing the school psychologist more. Things don't seem to be getting better. Mrs. Turner tells me that you don't say much in these sessions. I'd say it's time you truly start opening up and talking about how you feel. You both can continue to try to work through your problems together. That's what she's there for."

Violet arrived at school but paused and looked around before she got out of the car. Inside her mind she was wondering how she was going to press through the day. She was looking for a sign of hope to appear. She was trying to think of a reason for walking with her head held high that day but, sadly, couldn't think of anything. Violet knew she was in for a long day. Instead of turning to God, she turned to figuring out a way that she could get out of it.

Finally she got out of the car. Her mother said goodbye to her, but there was no reply from Violet. With her head toward the ground, she made her way to her classroom and didn't bother to greet any of her classmates or her teacher. Violet just sat down at her desk and put her head down. Her teacher knew what day it was and knew that she might be in for a long day as well.

Last year, on the day of the daddy-daughter dance, Violet had had an outburst in class. She started yelling and throwing things, and everyone had to clear out of the room. The principal and teacher had to restrain her. It was recommended that she stayed home for a week, and after that it had been mandatory for her to see the school psychologist. The students were scared of her after that and continued to be. Violet's teacher, Mrs. Summers, couldn't be scared of her, however. She had to be a part of the support group, like she'd been all year, so she took a deep breath and decided to check on Violet.

"Violet, how are we doing this morning?" Mrs. Summers approached Violet's desk.

Violet just kept her head down and didn't bother to reply.

"Have anything good for breakfast?"

Still there was no reply from Violet, and Mrs. Summers knew that she wasn't going to get anywhere right now.

"Look, I know this is a hard day for you. I just want you to know that if you need anything today, I'm here."

Mrs. Summers then walked away to start greeting the rest of the students coming in. She looked back in dismay at Violet; she didn't like to see any of her students in this much pain. She loved each and every single one of her students and knew that today she was going to have to demonstrate her love for Violet more than ever. Mrs. Summers just hoped that, sooner or later, Violet would be able to experience the joys of being a kid.

All the students were finally in the classroom and ready to go. The first thing the class did in the morning was math. That was Violet's favorite subject, and Mrs. Summers was trying to be optimistic. She hoped the math problems would get Violet going. There was a lady at the door, though. It was the school psychologist, Mrs. Turner, and she wanted to meet with Violet first thing in the morning. Even though Mrs. Summers wanted Violet to experience her favorite subject, she knew that her seeing the school psychologist right away was for the best, that talking out your problems was the best medicine. Mrs. Summers decided to save math for later; the students could start making their Father's Day cards.

"Violet, someone special is here to see you and wants you to go with her," Mrs. Summers indicated the school psychologist.

"This isn't what I had in mind for today," said Violet as she rolled her eyes.

Mrs. Turner then intervened. "The principal, Mrs. Summers, your mom, and I thought it would be best for you to see me first thing in the morning. We just want to help you."

"Fine! I'll go, but I'm not talking," Violet said with agitation in her voice.

Mrs. Turner and Violet made their way to her office. The goal of the session was to get Violet to talk or at least be open to ideas of how she could move forward in her life and develop skills to cope with what she was going through. Mrs. Turner was determined to break down the walls that Violet had built up over the preceding years, but she knew that it wasn't going to happen in one day. She was prepared to take baby steps with Violet, one session at a time.

"So, Violet, it has come to my attention from your support group that you haven't been acting like yourself lately. It seems like you're still in a bad place. You continue to not really eat or participate in class, and you hang out alone on the playground."

"Yeah, what about it?"

"It's not normal behavior for a kid. Kids should be playing, laughing, and trying to make friends. We're all concerned and just want to know what's going on in your mind. Let us help you."

"You really want to help me?"

"Of course, Violet."

"I want my father!"

"I get that life has been hard without your father, but the healing process can start today. If you want it to, that is."

"Did you not hear me? I want my father back!"

"We can only move forward and heal from here."

Violet abruptly interrupted Mrs. Turner. "Can we please be done here?" she said anxiously.

"But, Violet, we just started," Mrs. Turner replied.

"I said that I don't care to talk anymore."

"Well, Violet, we're here, so we should try to make the best of it."

Violet had enough of what Mrs. Turner was saying. There was a family photo on Mrs. Turner's desk, and Violet knew that it was one of Mrs. Turner's favorite possessions, so she went over to the desk, picked it up, and ripped it into pieces. Mrs. Turner just looked at her in awe, sadness in her face. Thoughts of hurt and confusion were going through her mind, but she knew she couldn't take any of Violet's acts personally right now, for she was in a very fragile stage. Mrs. Turner took Violet to the principal's office so they could see what appropriate action could be taken in response to Violet's behavior. Principal Stevens tried to engage Violet to see if he could get anything out of her, but she just sat there looking at the ground with her arms folded, so Mrs. Turner did the talking.

The first solution was to try to reach Violet's mom, but unfortunately, she was in a meeting and couldn't answer any calls. Principal Stevens kept in mind what had happened last year. The goal was to avoid a repeat, so he came up with an alternate solution—Violet would go back to class, and Mrs. Turner would keep an eye on her. Little did they know the solution wouldn't be enough and things would just end up getting worse as the day went on. Violet was a ticking time bomb just waiting to go off, and all these years of pain, grief, and confusion would end up coming out in the worst kind of way.

At around eleven in the morning, Violet wanted to return to class, so Mrs. Turner took her there. When they had arrived at the classroom, Violet didn't make eye contact with anyone and just rushed to her seat. Mrs. Summers was worried for Violet, but she knew that there was only an hour left of class before lunch, so it wouldn't be too bad for her to be there. While she was gone, the other students had finished making their Father's Day cards, so that was one less potential trigger for Violet. And on the bright side, it was time for math, Violet's favorite subject. Mrs. Summers was going to attempt to get Violet involved, but this never happened. Violet may have been back in that classroom physically, but she wasn't there mentally, a state that would continue for the rest of the day.

It was now noon and time for the kids to go to lunch. Violet didn't want to go with the rest of the class, but instead she wanted to eat lunch in Mrs. Turner's office, where there was peace and quiet. Violet headed to the comfy zone in Mrs. Turner's office, a space with a soft bean bag chair and a small table, to eat her lunch. Violet opened her lunchbox and saw that her mom had written a note: "Love you to the moon and back." This was the special way that Violet and her mother told each other "I love you." The note put a little smile on Violet's face, and Mrs. Turner saw that as an opportunity to have a conversation with Violet.

"It's really nice of your mom to put notes in your lunch. Does she do that every day?" asked Mrs. Turner.

"She does," replied Violet.

"That's really touching. Your mother must really love you."

"I guess," grumbled Violet.

"Why would you say, 'I guess'?"

"I don't like it when she talks about how much God loves me and that I should lean on him for comfort."

"So you think she doesn't love you because she won't stop telling you that?"

"No. It's just that…I don't like being lied to. How can someone who loves you just stand by and watch you be in so much pain? As far as I know, it's just some fairytale."

Mrs. Turner's heart was broken by what she was hearing. She was a Christian herself and wanted to tell Violet so much right then and there, but as someone who worked in education, she wasn't allowed to talk about God with students. Mrs. Turner couldn't even tell Violet that she would pray for her so that she might find peace and comfort. Instead, when the bell rang and it was time for them both to go back to class, she told Violet that she would be in her thoughts.

As the bell rang, Violet sighed because she knew it was time to go back to class. The morning was really rough for her and, quite frankly, she was just ready for the day to be over. Mrs. Turner expressed to Violet that there was no rush and that she could take her time if she wanted to. This gave Violet some relief because she didn't know if she could tolerate the day any longer.

Violet told Mrs. Turner that she wanted to take the long way back and stop at the bathroom. Violet kept silent the entire time she was walking. It was like she was in her own little world, trying to escape the realities of life. One could only wonder what was going on in her mind. However she did stop and take a look at all the neat decorations in the first-grade hallway. Since it was close to summer vacation, the first-grade hallway had a summer theme. This intrigued Violet and made her even more absentminded. What got her attention the most were the pictures that were hung up on each classroom bulletin board showing students riding their bikes, playing outside, or with their families on vacation. Violet was fascinated by one of the pictures and just kept staring and staring. Mrs. Turner tried getting her attention, but nothing.

"Violet...Violet...Violet," said Mrs. Turner repeatedly.

Violet finally snapped out of it and responded, "What... what is it?"

"Is everything okay? You blanked out for a minute," Mrs. Turner said with a concerned look on her face.

"Sure, I need to stop and use the bathroom, and then we can go back to class," Violet responded anxiously.

Violet frantically bolted to the bathroom and locked herself in the last stall. She was freaking out and trying to make sense of what had happened. The picture that had caught her eye had lit up with a glimmer of light, and it was as if the people in the photo had come to life. She swore that she could've walked right into the picture if she wanted to. It just seemed that real. She didn't want to say anything to Mrs. Turner because she might think Violet was crazy. Violet didn't know if it was because she was tired or stressed, but she just dismissed it like any other thought she had. Ten minutes had gone by, and Violet didn't want to keep Mrs. Turner waiting any longer, so she went to the sink, threw water on her face, and went back into the hallway.

"Everything okay?" Mrs. Turner asked.

"Let's just get back to class and get this over with," replied Violet.

When Violet arrived at the classroom, she did the same thing as she had done in the morning, which was just sit there with a blank expression on her face. Mrs. Summers and the rest of the class all had concerned looks on their faces and were worried about what might happen next. Was Violet going to snap again? I mean, she had an episode in the morning and hadn't seemed to really recover after that. The best thing to do, though, was to just let Violet be and get through the rest of the afternoon. Her sitting there, left to her thoughts, was a lot better than what had happened this morning.

Violet grew restless as the hours went on. She kept looking at the clock and hoping that it was 3:45 p.m., so she could pack up and go home. The more she looked at the clock, the slower time went by, and the slower that time went by, the more impatient and anxious she grew. It was as if everyone was frozen in time. Violet just really wanted to go home to be alone in her room; she didn't know how much longer she could handle this.

All of a sudden, Violet started shaking, sweating, and breathing heavily. These were the signs of a nervous breakdown—a fact that Mrs. Summers and Mrs. Turner noted as they worried about what was going to happen next. Mrs. Turner knew she had to act soon and remove Violet from the situation, but it was too late. Violet had enough and stormed out of the room in a fit of rage. She then proceeded to go from bulletin board to bulletin board, tearing off all the daddy-daughter dance flyers and yelling at the top of her lungs. Mrs. Turner tried to stop her but had no luck in doing so. Mrs. Summers had to leave her classroom so she could attend to the chaos that was ensuing in the hallway.

"Violet, you have to snap out of it. It's not worth it. You're only going to hurt yourself," Mrs. Summers said.

"*I hate this stupid daddy-daughter dance, and I hate all of you!*" screamed Violet.

"Violet, please! You're scaring the other kids," responded Mrs. Summers.

"Leave me alone…You don't know what it's like…I just want to go home and forget about everything," cried Violet.

Following Violet's episode, the rest of the class was terrified. Mrs. Summers knew that she had no choice but to stop class and hold a meeting on the carpet to address what had happened. Not only that, but she also knew she was going to have to send emails out to all the parents about the event that had taken place.

"Friends, I need your full and undivided attention. What I'm about to say is very important," said Mrs. Summers.

"This is about Violet, isn't it?" replied Mikey.

"I'm scared of her," said Ashley.

"She's not coming back in here, is she?" said Susie.

"No, she's not, but may I remind you about the contract we all signed at the beginning of the year? What was the most important thing on there?" Mrs. Summers said with frustration in her voice.

"Be kind to one another, and always be a friend," replied the class.

"Class, some friends need help more than others. Some friends have bad days. Even I have bad days. We have to be there for Violet. She's really hurting on the inside," said Mrs. Summers.

"We should make her cards, and you can give them to her at the end of the day," said Eric.

"That's a great idea! She'll love it. Great thinking, team!"

As her classmates prepared the cards, Violet had to sit with Mrs. Turner in her office until the end of the day. Considering the fact that Principal Stevens's solution hadn't worked out well, it was for the best. Violet went over to her normal spot in Mrs. Turner's office, got her cassette player out, and listened to the song "Here Comes the Sun" by the Beatles.

When Violet was little, she heard this song on the radio during one of the long car rides she and her mom used to take. She fell in love with it instantly, and her mom ended up getting her a cassette tape with the song on it for her sixth birthday. This was Violet's go-to song to calm down when she was feeling anxious and out of sorts.

During this time she fell asleep and had a dream. Violet was in her attic at home, and she saw the same glimmer of light that had been emitted by the picture in the hallway. This time the light was shining down on a dresser. Violet went over to the dresser to check it out, and then one of the drawers slid open a bit by itself. She pulled the drawer out the rest of the way and discovered a shoebox. As Violet began to open the shoebox in her dream, she was awoken by Mrs. Turner. It was time to go home, and Violet's mom was waiting for her at the office.

This wasn't the first time that Violet's mom had been called into the office. Violet had completely shut down over the years and was always finding different ways to get out of school and doing her work. Violet was not only causing problems at school, but also causing problems at home. They used to bond together—go get ice cream, watch movies, go to the park, and be there for each other—but the bond had soured over the years. As time went on, Violet became distant and angry at her mother. Mrs. Cooper was helpless and wanted answers and guidance on how she could regain the close relationship she once had with Violet and be a part of her support group.

Violet saw her mom standing there with a look of displeasure on her face. Violet's mom had heard what had happened and was beyond sad about it. Between her stressful job, keeping up with the payments for the house, and providing for Violet, who was acting out again, she just didn't know what to do. Jennifer Cooper was a social worker for the city of Orlando. Jennifer's job was to try to help kids get removed from unstable households so they could end up in a healthy environment and have a chance at a better life. She'd always had a big heart when it came to helping others. Jennifer wasn't an expert in childhood trauma, but she still wanted to help her beloved Violet out to the best of her ability.

She told Violet to wait in the office while she spoke with Principal Stevens, Mrs. Summers, and Mrs. Turner.

"I'm really sorry about what happened today. I should've come and gotten her after the first time she acted out," Violet's mom said expressively.

"It's okay, Mrs. Cooper. We understand that this is a difficult time for Violet, and you have our full support," said Principal Stevens.

"The objective of this meeting is to figure out a plan going forward so Violet can feel at peace with her situation," interjected Mrs. Turner.

"My heart hurts from what I witnessed today. I don't want to have to experience that again. Also, could you please give these to Violet? Our class made cards for her, and we really do hope these cheer her up," said Mrs. Summers.

"Thank you so much! That's really nice of you, considering today's circumstances. What is the plan going forward, though?" said Mrs. Cooper.

"We think that Violet should see Mrs. Turner every day until there's progress," replied Principal Stevens.

"And once we see progress, then we will decrease the frequency of the sessions. The ultimate goal is for Violet to find closure as well as coping skills going forward so she can resume a normal life," added Mrs. Turner.

"Is there anything I can do? What's my role in this?" replied Mrs. Cooper.

"As for today, I think it's best you stay neutral. Going forward, be there for moral support, bond with her, and try to get her to open up more, but don't force her to talk if she doesn't want to. She'll open up when the time is right," said Mrs. Turner.

"But why is she acting like this toward me? I'm her mother! Does she resent me for what happened with her father? Does she hold me responsible?" replied Mrs. Cooper.

"Mrs. Cooper, we won't know until she opens up more. We can only trust the process for now," said Mrs. Turner.

The agreement was made that Violet was to see Mrs. Turner each school day first thing in the morning. Mrs. Cooper knew that Violet wasn't going to like this one bit, but she knew that it was necessary. Violet's treatment with Mrs. Turner needed to work this time. It just had to work because Mrs. Cooper wasn't sure what she was going to do if it didn't. Mrs. Cooper then approached Violet and told her to grab her things. She tried to clasp Violet's hand, but Violet just pulled away. Tears started rolling down Mrs. Cooper's face, but then she remembered what Mrs. Turner had said "when the time is right" and was able to hold back her crying.

As they walked to the car, a group of girls waited with their dads by the gym for the dance to start. Mrs. Cooper did her best to distract Violet from witnessing this, but it was too late. Violet suddenly stopped walking and just stood there with her fists balled up, looking like she was about to explode. The feeling of anger was quickly overwhelmed by sadness, and Violet fell to the ground, bawling her eyes out. Most parents wouldn't have wanted to make a scene and just picked up their kid and left, but Mrs. Cooper again remembered what Mrs. Turner had said about being there for moral support, so she consoled her daughter and started to cry with her. She tried to reassure her that everything was going to be all right.

"It hurts so much, Mom. Please make it stop," Violet cried uncontrollably.

"If I could take away all your pain and transfer it to me, I would," her mother said.

"Why can't Dad just come home, so we can all be a family again?" Violet whimpered.

"Violet, everything will feel better over time. We all love you dearly and are here to help."

"How can you say that? It's been four years, and I don't feel any better than I did after the first. I'm not okay, and I don't know if I'll ever be."

"Violet, let's just go home. We can talk more in the car or when we get home…I mean, that's if you want to."

Violet still didn't really care to talk; that's how it had been all day. Instead Violet just stared out the window the entire way home. She had so much going through her mind. *Why is this happening to me? Why can't I be like the rest of the kids?* It was like her brain was on a hamster wheel that would never slow down. Violet was just a kid, and her heart was supposed to be full of joy and carefree, but instead it was full of sorrow and plagued with grief. She tried so hard to relax and calm down but kept weeping. Something did catch her eye on the way home, though. There it was again, that flash of light that she had seen twice today, and this time it was shining on the words "new beginnings" on a sign on the bus next to them. Just like that, Violet stopped crying, and she was calm. There was something about those words that gave Violet this feeling of relief, but she couldn't make anything of it quite yet.

Violet's mom pulled into the driveway, and Violet didn't hesitate to get out of the car. She bolted for the door, went inside, and headed straight to her room. Her mom wanted to talk with her about the plan that everyone at school had come up with but knew it could wait for later. This would also give Violet time to cool off, and maybe she wouldn't take the news badly. Mrs. Cooper started getting dinner ready and yelled up to Violet that it would be ready in a half hour. Meanwhile, Violet was lying in her bed, trying to make sense of what had happened today. Her thoughts weren't focused as much on her actions, but more on the significance of her dream and the light shining down on the picture and words. This light had to be of some importance—was it a sign? Was someone or something trying to show her something? Before she could go further with her own questions, she heard her mom calling her to come down for dinner. Violet said she wasn't hungry, but her mom insisted.

When Violet got to the table, her mom didn't waste any time and proceeded to tell her about the plan going forward. As expected, Violet didn't like what she heard, and an argument ensued.

"What do you mean I have to go talk with her every day?" asked Violet.

"It's for the best. What's the worst that could happen?" replied her mom.

"Well, maybe I'm not ready to talk yet."

"You don't have to talk…you can just listen," replied Mrs. Cooper. "Ask God for guidance through this as well and listen to that too."

"As far as I'm concerned, there is no God."

"Sweetie, how can you say that?"

"Well, where is he, Mom? I've never seen him or heard him," Violet said facetiously.

"Remember that believing isn't seeing. We don't walk by sight, but by faith."

"My faith is gone, Mom, and I'll never believe," said Violet with anger in her voice.

"But Vio—"

Before Jennifer could get another word out, Violet picked up her dinner plate, threw it against the wall, and ran upstairs. Jennifer was in complete shock and just sat there in disbelief. She buried her head deep into her folded arms and couldn't hold back her tears. Her poor little girl was in so much pain and didn't know what to do or how any of this was going to work out. She felt like she was running out of time and was losing her daughter more and more each day.

Jennifer started pacing the kitchen. She then stopped by the sliding glass door in the kitchen and took a look outside in the backyard. Memories of how she and her daughter used to play outside popped into her head, and then the memories of when her husband was around entered too. Running around in the backyard, playing monkey in the middle, and having squirt gun fights were the days that Jennifer longed to have back. She missed her husband and the times they would sit outside after they tucked Violet in and talked for hours. Some nights he would surprise her with a candle-lit dinner under the moon and stars when they had their occasional date nights. Most importantly, she missed the times they had together as a family and would give anything to have that back.

Before Mrs. Cooper went to her room, she went to go pay Violet a visit to check on how she was doing. Even though Violet wasn't always in the best mood, Jennifer still really loved her daughter and was determined to get their relationship back on track. She entered the room and right away, Violet wanted her to leave, but Jennifer refused. Even though Mrs. Turner told her to stay neutral, in good conscience she just couldn't do that.

"Violet, what have I done to you? Please talk to me. I love you."

"You really don't know after all this time?"

"No, I don't. Please help me understand."

"You keep telling me to move on like it's nothing. Maybe it was easy for you to move on, but I'm not ready."

"Wait a minute...That's not fair. You have no idea how I feel. We can't keep dwelling in the past though. I need you here with me."

"I don't want to move forward. I want my dad."

"Well, I want my Violet back."

"She's gone, Mom, and you're wasting your time."

"But, Violet..."

"I don't love you anymore. Leave me alone."

"Honey, you don't mean that. You're just really upset."

"Yes, I do."

"I'm sorry to hear that, Violet. I'll always love you no matter what."

It felt like a sharp knife had pierced Jennifer's heart at the sound of those words, and she abruptly left Violet's room and headed to hers. As she was walking toward her room, she started looking to God for answers but didn't hear anything at that moment. When she got into her room, she lay down and started thinking of what Mrs. Turner had said about time and patience. At that moment she knew those two words had God written all over them. She was going to have to be patient and trust in God's timing.

Violet didn't have God; all she had was a broken heart that was tainted with feelings of anger, guilt, shame, and sadness. She felt completely alone in the world with no one to turn to. The more she thought about her dad, the more it weighed on her heart. She never really liked to talk about her father and suppressed those memories so she didn't have to feel any pain. She was stuck in the denial stage of grieving. Violet wasn't ready to let go and accept that her father was gone. Violet's mom never really talked about her dad either. Was it because she was hurting on the inside too? Was she not ready to talk either? Whatever the reason, Violet was going to have to find a way to deal with her current situation, emotions and stop running from the truth.

Violet paused for a minute and remembered the dream she had about the shoebox in her attic. She sprang out of bed and headed for the stairs that led to the attic. There it was—the dresser that was in her dream as well. Violet ran over to the dresser and pulled open the exact same drawer; before her eyes was the shoebox.

Violet opened the shoebox. Inside were old photos and some newspaper articles. It was all her dad's stuff that had been collected over the years from when he was a child to the last day he was alive, at her birthday party. The photo that stood out to Violet the most was one of her dad, mom, and her on that fourth birthday. They looked so happy, and that made Violet want her family to be whole again even more. There was another picture that caught her eye, but she had to pick it up to get a good look. It was a picture of her dad as a kid, about her age now. Violet couldn't help but smile at this photo. Her dad looked so happy and alive; she wished she were able to feel the same. The overwhelming emotions caused tears to fall from her face onto the photo, and the light she had seen throughout the day appeared again. The boy in the photo came to life, and it seemed he was signaling for her to come into the photo. Violet thought she was dreaming, so she pinched herself, but she was indeed awake. She was scared, but then there were those words again: *new beginnings*.

Two

The attic was now filled with a bright light that was coming from the photo. The picture came to life just like the photo did in the hallway of Violet's school. Violet stood there in deep thought, contemplating if this photo served as a portal and where it was going to take her. Could this world be the key to help her find "new beginnings"? The boy in the picture was once again signaling and reaching his hand out for her to come in, but Violet was still unsure if she should extend her hand.

The portal looked like it was about to close, so at the very last moment, Violet stuck her hand in the photo of her dad as a kid at the beach and was sucked in. It seemed so unreal to Violet that this was happening. She pinched herself again to see if she was dreaming, but this was all definitely real. Violet was actually at the same beach as her dad was in the photograph. It was a beach in North Carolina called Lake Lure Beach. It was so nice and warm. The scenery was so gorgeous to Violet. The sun was shining down on the sand that added a sparkle to it. There was a nice cool breeze that made the heat more tolerable, and the white waves were crashing on the shore.

Violet wanted to find her dad. She started walking down the beach and right away saw a group of kids in the distance.

She looked a little closer, and there was her dad. Violet couldn't contain her excitement and started running toward him to give him a hug. When she got to her dad, she embraced him. Violet's dad pulled away because he was confused as to why a complete stranger would just come up to him and give him a hug. Violet was disappointed when he first pulled away but then realized that even though she knew that this was her dad, he had no idea that Violet was going to be his daughter one day.

"Do I know you?" asked Violet's dad.

"No, I don't think you do," replied Violet. "But you will one day."

"Then why did you run up to me and give me a hug?"

"Sorry about that. I must've mistaken you for someone I hadn't seen in a while and got really excited. My name's Violet. What's yours?"

"My name's Tommy, and these are my friends, Brian, Joey, Samantha, John, and Melissa. You want to play with us?"

"Sure! What are we playing?" asked Violet.

"Tag, you're it!" exclaimed Tommy.

"Catch us if you can," Brian added.

Violet was so excited that she was going to get to play with her dad. She had always dreamed of getting to play with him again like she used to in her backyard when she was a toddler; this was her chance to make up for lost time. Violet didn't bother trying to chase any of the other kids, focusing only on Tommy. Tommy was the fastest of them all and was really confident that no one could ever catch him. He was known as the king of tag, but little did he know Violet had some speed in her as well. Tommy thought he had a big lead, but when he looked back, Violet was right behind him and really close to tagging him. Tommy couldn't believe it and started to pick up the pace. Violet kicked it into second gear as well and at last tagged Tommy. All the kids looked at each other, stunned, and just like that, Tommy's streak was over.

The game concluded, but Violet was confused because not everyone had been tagged. It turned out that in this game of tag, if you tagged the champion first, you automatically won. All the kids were impressed and told Violet that she could hang with them anytime. She didn't know what to say because she had never experienced this in her life, but now she was getting a taste of what it was like to have friends and be a carefree kid. All she could do was smile and nod. Now that the game was over, Brian mentioned he was hungry, and everyone else all felt the same way and agreed that they should get food. There was a food stand that served good hotdogs and fries, so they all headed there. Violet was hungry as well but didn't have any money to buy food, but Tommy ended up offering to buy for her.

"Your parents didn't give you money for food?" asked Tommy.

"Maybe she doesn't have parents," Samantha chimed in.

"You an orphan or something?" asked Brian.

"Brian! That's none of your business, and, plus, we just met Violet," Melissa added.

"No, it's okay. I do have parents, but we don't have much money," Violet replied.

Tommy stepped in. "That's okay. I'll buy you some food."

"You really don't have to. I'll just eat later."

"Nonsense. I never let my friends go hungry."

"Maybe we could come over to play and meet your parents sometime, Violet,"Brian offered.

"Brian, I know I've heard your parents tell you to not invite yourself over to other people's houses…it's rude," said Tommy.

"Yeah, Brian, have some manners," the rest of the group added.

Violet didn't know what to say at that moment. She knew that she didn't have parents here, but she couldn't tell them that. Violet also realized that she couldn't tell them about how she got sucked into a picture of Tommy and somehow ended up here. They wouldn't believe her and would think she was crazy. As Violet paused, thinking about what to say, she noticed this woman in the distance waving at her, but she didn't wave back because she remembered what her mom had told her about strangers. It was very odd to her, though, that the woman was trying to get her attention. Still, Violet didn't bother to acknowledge her and rejoined the conversation with her friends.

"My parents never let me have anybody over," Violet said.

"*Lame!*" replied Brian.

"Brian!" shouted the group.

"What? What type of parents doesn't let their kids' friends over to their house?"

Just out of curiosity, Violet looked up at the woman to see if she was still there. The woman was standing on a dock, looking as though she was enjoying the view. It seemed she had been there for quite a while. Violet thought she could've been waiting for someone, but was it for her? It couldn't have been. Why would a complete stranger wait for someone she's never met? As Violet was going to shift her attention back to the group, the same light she had seen before was there again, shining down on the woman. The group noticed that Violet was in a daze and tried to get her attention.

"Violet…Earth to Violet…come in, Violet," said Tommy.

There was no response, but Violet started to walk away without saying a word of goodbye.

"Where is she going?" asked Samantha.

"I have no clue," said Melissa.

"Violet, come back!" Joey shouted.

Violet still didn't respond and kept walking. Tommy knew they were all going to hang out later at the secret hideout but wanted Violet to come, so he yelled out the plans to her.

"Hey, Violet, if you're interested, we're all going to meet up here later to ride our bikes down to our secret hangout spot. Hope to see you back here."

"You think she heard you?" Brian asked.

"We'll only know if she shows up," said Tommy.

"She's a weird one, but a good kind of weird," said John.

"Yeah, she is, isn't she?"

Tommy was intrigued by Violet. Who was this girl? It was just so odd that they had crossed paths like this. There had to be a deeper reason why this had happened. Tommy thought about Violet's big hug, about the fact that it had come out of nowhere. Maybe it was fate that they crossed paths because maybe Violet didn't have any friends and needed a friend or two. Whatever the reason was, he still wanted to show Violet a really good time. Tommy just accepted that it was fate, shrugged it off, and continued on with his friends.

Meanwhile, Violet started walking toward the mysterious woman on the dock. She was curious to see who this woman was and why she was trying to get her attention. Violet noticed that the lady was really enjoying the sunset and didn't want to bother her, so she just sat at the end of the dock, took off her shoes, and put her feet in the water. Violet really enjoyed sunsets. They had a calming effect and brought her to a happy place. The mysterious woman noticed how much Violet was enjoying the beauty of the sunset, and it reminded her of her own enjoyment of sunsets as a child. Aside from that, the mysterious woman realized she had a job to do and was going to carry it out in exactly the way she'd been instructed.

"This is such a nice sunset," the mysterious woman said in Violet's direction.

"Yeah, you could say that again," replied Violet.

"I've been coming down here to watch sunsets since I was a little girl like you."

"I'm new here, so this is my first time. I really do like sunsets, though," said Violet. "If you don't mind me asking, what's your name?"

"It's Lucy, but everyone around here calls me Mom."

"So everyone calls you Mom? But why?"

"I love and care for people around here. When someone is in need, I'm there."

"By the way, I saw that you didn't come here with your parents, and the friends you were with just left you. It looks like you don't have anywhere to go."

Violet wanted to lie to the mysterious woman and feed her the same story that she had given to her friends—that she did indeed have parents, and they were waiting for her to get home, just like the families of her new friends. For some reason, though, she got this feeling that she shouldn't lie and that she would be in good hands if she told the truth. Violet decided she would do the right thing and tell the mysterious woman the truth but would leave the detail about the photograph out. That's one thing she felt was a good idea to keep to herself.

"No, I don't have parents, and I definitely don't have a place to stay."

"Well, that's all right. You can stay with me. I have an extra room all set up, and there's plenty of food. You will get to meet my husband, Mark, as well."

"I don't know what to say...you're too kind."

"They don't call me Mom for nothing."

"If we somehow run into my friends, could you act like my real parents?" Violet asked. "I kind of lied to them and said I had parents, and when they asked if they could come over sometime, I told them that my parents don't like having people over so they wouldn't find out the truth."

"Of course, dear! Your secret's safe with me," said Lucy. "We should also have your friends over sometime. I would love to meet them. Now let's go. My husband is going to meet us for a meal at this restaurant we really like."

Violet was still kind of skeptical about going with this woman. The thought of going off and living with two complete strangers went against everything that almost every single adult had told her (i.e., "Don't talk to strangers"). But there was something different about this woman that had Violet reconsidering what she was told. The woman who was referred to as Mom had this loving and comforting vibe about her. It was the exact same vibe that her real mom gave off. This really was a telling sign to Violet that this woman meant well and that she should try to trust her.

Violet continued to walk with Lucy to the restaurant, which was only a couple of blocks away. Violet asked her what restaurant they were going to, and Lucy said that there was this place called the Old Town Diner that she and her husband really liked. Old Town Diner was a restaurant in the small town of Spindale, North Carolina. Violet had never seen a town so small before because she was from the big city of Orlando, Florida, which consisted of a massive population. Plus, it was a big tourist attraction year-round. This was a big step down from what she was used to, but she liked how peaceful and quiet it was. There were a lot of small businesses and convenience stores bunched up together and not that many roads, so it was easy to navigate.

Violet mentioned that she had already eaten at Lake Lure Beach, but Lucy said that was fine and she could just get dessert. Violet and Lucy arrived at the diner, walked in, and joined Lucy's husband, Mark, who was sitting in a booth by the window. Lucy introduced Violet to Mark, and Violet could feel that same loving vibe that was coming off of Lucy. Violet was smiling and really happy on the inside because not only was this too good to be true, but everything seemed normal, calm, and peaceful now.

The waitress brought them menus and, after a few minutes, asked them if they were ready to order. Lucy told the waitress that they needed a minute or two to figure out what they wanted. In the meantime, she had the waitress bring them drinks. Lucy got an iced tea; she ordered Mark a Coke and

Violet chocolate milk. This was Violet's favorite, but how did this lady know? Violet had just met her not too long ago, and she was already able to pick out her favorite drink. Could it be that she just assumed all kids liked chocolate milk? Violet couldn't turn down free chocolate milk, so she happily enjoyed it and proceeded to tell Lucy and Mark about her day at the beach.

"I had a lot of fun. I met six new friends today. Their names are Tommy, Brian, Melissa, Joey, John and Samantha."

"Well, what did you do?" asked Lucy and Mark.

"We played a game of tag. It was so much fun!" Violet responded with excitement. "The boy named Tommy is known as the best tag player, and I tagged him. Now I'm known as the new champion."

"Good for you. We're so happy that you made some new friends today."

"Oh, yeah. And one more thing: Tommy and the rest of the gang are meeting back at the beach later today to hang out some more. They told me that they wanted to show me their secret hangout spot."

"That should be really fun. Just make sure you're home at a reasonable hour," said Lucy.

"Where is home?"

"Mark is better at directions than me, so he'll tell you."

Mark pulled out a map for Violet and explained how to get back to their house from the beach. "All right, so here's the parking lot. You're going to turn left out of the parking lot, head down two blocks, and make a right. From there you'll see a stop sign on the left, and we're two houses down from the sign."

"Could you please repeat that?"

"I'll do you one better. I'll trace the route you'll take to get home, and you can take this map with you. We would hate to see you get lost. After all, our job is to keep you safe," Mark added.

"Thanks, I really appreciate it. I have to run to the bathroom, though, so could you both order for me in case I'm not here when the waitress gets back?" asked Violet.

"Sure thing! Strawberry waffles with whip cream on top it is!" said Lucy.

"How did you know that?"

"Know what?"

"Um, nothing. I'll be right back," said Violet.

As Violet was walking to the bathroom, she kept looking back at Lucy and Mark in amazement. This all seemed so unreal. Not only were they the most hospitable and loving strangers she'd ever met, but they had just ordered her favorite food in the whole wide world. The only person on earth who knew this fact, until then, was her real mom. Who were these people, and why were they being so nice? *They don't even know me, but they could sense that there was something wrong and opened up their house to me. I feel so special and loved right now.* As Violet kept questioning this, the word "trust" popped up in her mind. It seemed so crazy to trust two complete strangers, but for some reason, it seemed right. Violet decided to fully embrace them and stop being skeptical. Violet finished washing her hands and decided to rejoin them at the booth.

"How long until you're going to meet your friends back at Lake Lure Beach?" asked Lucy.

"In about an hour."

"Then we better hurry up and finish eating. We wouldn't want you to be late for your playdate with your new friends," said Lucy.

"Where did you say you all were going again?" asked Mark.

"Tommy said that we're going to ride our bikes down this trail that leads to this secret hangout."

"Oh, yeah! There's a trail surrounded by woods that leads to a hidden lake. There's a rope that you can use to swing yourself into the lake. It's a lot of fun," Mark replied.

"How did you..." But before Violet could finish asking them how they knew about the secret hangout spot, she remembered that she had vowed to stop being skeptical of everything, and so she asked a different question. "I'm guessing you both went there when you were kids?"

"Yeah, we did. It was the highlight of our summers until we got older," said Mark.

"Those were the good ole days," added Lucy.

They all finished eating. Mark paid the bill and headed for the door. It looked like it was about to get dark soon. They had about three hours of sunlight left, so Violet wanted to hurry and not waste a bit of sunlight. She started running back to the beach. Lucy and Mark told her to slow down, but she couldn't contain her excitement and kept going. This was Violet's first big adventure, and she couldn't wait to see what was in store. A bike ride and taking a swim on this hot summer's day sounded pretty refreshing. Violet then looked back at Lucy and Mark and told them to hurry up, so they started running too. They weren't young anymore and would've preferred walking, but they knew how much this meant to Violet, so they did the best they could to keep up.

Three

Violet was in for quite the adventure with her dad and the rest of the group. She'd never been to a secret hangout before, so her body was tingling with excitement. Sadly, she'd never been a part of a secret in general because she didn't have friends back home to share them with. This was going to be Violet's first chance to experience firsthand what the joys of having friends consisted of.

When they got to the beach, the group was all waiting on their bikes and was surprised to see Violet. They had assumed Violet wasn't going to show up, but to their amazement, there she was. Violet then realized that she was missing an important component of this activity, which was a bike. She looked back at Lucy and Mark in disappointment because she didn't know what she was going to do. They told her that it looked like there was room on Tommy's bike and encouraged her to ask if she could hitch a ride. Violet then said goodbye to Lucy and Mark and thanked them for everything they'd done so far. Lucy and Mark told her not to worry about it and expressed that help would always be there whenever she needed it. Violet gave them both a big hug and proceeded to head over to the group.

Everyone was glad that Violet had made it but noticed that she didn't have a bike. That was okay, though, because Tommy, indeed, had extra space on his bike and offered to give Violet a ride. Tommy told Violet that she should hang on because to them everything was a race, and they wanted to race down the gravel trail to the secret hangout spot. They all lined up at the starting line.

Joey said, "On your mark, get set, go!"

Then they were off. Violet had never raced on a bike before, so she was scared and decided to close her eyes. She did like the wind touching her face and going through her hair. The feeling reminded her of the car rides that she, her mom, and their dog Buster used to take. Buster would be on Violet's lap, sticking his head out the window. Once in a while, her mom would let Violet stick her head out the window too. Buster had been a source of comfort when Violet was younger, so thinking of him made her feel safe again.

They finally reached the hangout spot, and to no one's surprise, Tommy won the race. The prize for the winner was first use of the swing. The kids hopped off their bikes and started heading toward the water. Violet was wondering if they had bathing suits, but to her amazement they all just jumped in with their clothes on. Violet didn't want to get her clothes wet, so she didn't go in with them. The group was yelling for her to come in: "Who cares if you get your clothes wet? They'll just air dry during the bike ride home. Plus you have to live a little."

Violet couldn't disagree with that, so she started to run toward the water and jumped right in. She went all the way to the bottom and had a chance to look around. The water was so clear, and the sun reflecting on the water made it look really beautiful. Violet started running out of breath, so she made her way to the surface.

"Wow, this is quite a hangout you guys have here. The water is so refreshing," said Violet.

"Yup! This is our slice of paradise," Tommy responded.

"We hang out here every summer and have created some great memories here," added Samantha.

"Speaking of memories, remember when Brian swung from the rope into the water and lost his bathing suit?" Joey asked with laughter in his voice.

"That was hilarious!" Melissa offered.

"What a classic moment!" added John.

"Ha, ha, very funny," said Brian sarcastically. "I would like to swing off the rope soon. So, Tommy, how about you go ahead and take your turn?"

Tommy got out of the water and went over to the rope, which hung from the branch of a tall oak tree by the water. Violet got butterflies in her stomach just watching Tommy head over to swing into the water. She'd never done that before, so she was nervous about trying it. She was also amazed at how fearless Tommy was. Earlier, he was riding his bike, not even worrying about the speed as he was going downhill or heading around turns, and now he was about to swing from a high up branch into the water. Tommy had to be the bravest kid she'd ever met. He was about to leap but paused and looked at Violet. He insisted on giving his turn to her. She told Tommy she didn't know how to swing on a rope, and he told her he would show her.

"All right, just hold on here tightly, count to three, and go."

"How about you go first, and I'll watch how you do it?"

"Nonsense. We'll go together."

Violet and Tommy each grabbed a part of the rope and backed up to get a running start. He looked at her to confirm she was ready. Violet gave him a small nod, but Tommy realized he had forgotten an important part of the instructions—that at the highest point she needed to let go of the rope to get more air and avoid hurting her hands. He brought Violet up to speed and told her he would say the word "now" when it was time to let go. Even though she was jumping with Tommy, Violet was pretty nervous, but she knew she couldn't back out now. Both of them ran as fast as they could and made their way to the edge of the hill. Before Violet knew it, they were in mid-air. Violet looked over at Tommy and could see the joy in his face. She thought to herself, *Wow, Tommy and his friends sure know how to live*, but the thought was interrupted by Tommy's signal word. They both let go and plunged into the water, reaching the bottom. Both of them swam to the top quickly, and when they rose to the surface, Tommy gave Violet a high five. This made Violet feel really good—and alive as well, for once.

"Wow! You guys really got some air," said Joey.

"I'd give them a ten out of ten," added Melissa and John.

"Not too bad," said Brian.

"See, Violet, I knew you could do it," said Tommy.

"That was so much fun. Thanks for showing me, Tommy," Violet had happiness and excitement in her voice.

"No problem, Violet. Just know that you don't have to do everything alone. There are always friends there to help you through it, if you want them to," responded Tommy.

Violet was really experiencing the full joys of being a kid at this moment, but she was also wondering what it would be like when she had to go home. She had this feeling that she couldn't stay in this time forever. Violet decided that she would worry about that later and just live in the moment.

The group continued to have such a good time at the secret spot, taking multiple turns swinging off the rope into the water, playing Marco Polo, racing from one side of the lake to the other, even playing tag in the water. Before they knew it, it was time to head back.

Violet mentioned to Tommy that she was going to need someone to take her home; she added that her parents had invited the children to come by and visit sometime. The group was surprised because they remembered that she said her parents didn't like having people over, but Violet explained that her parents had a sudden change of heart when she told them about her new friends. Melissa added that they should all take Violet home so they could meet her parents tonight. Violet didn't know if that was a good idea, but they insisted. Plus they all wanted to make sure Violet got home okay. The group wanted to race home, but Violet just wanted to go slow and try to enjoy the ride this time. She hoped that Lucy and Mark wouldn't be too upset that she was bringing people over on such short notice.

At last they arrived at Lucy and Mark's house, and Violet told the group to wait outside while she went and talked to them. Before she went in, Tommy mentioned that they should all have a sleepover in the backyard. The group called it an "old-fashioned campout." It was also a tradition they practiced every summer. Violet told them that she would see what she could do but made no promises. She made her way inside and told Lucy and Mark that the group was waiting outside and wanted to know if they could all have a sleepover in the back-yard. Lucy and Mark didn't even hesitate before saying it was all right. They then came to the door and welcomed everyone in, telling them to make themselves comfy while they set everything up in the backyard.

"For a mom and dad you said didn't like having anyone over, they sure are nice," exclaimed Tommy.

"They even offered to set everything up in the backyard for us!" added Brian.

"Do you think they have marshmallows, graham crackers, and chocolate bars so we can make s'mores?" Samantha and Melissa asked.

"You just read my mind," said John.

"You know what else we can do with the marshmallows?" said Joey.

"What?" asked Violet.

"I have three words: Chubby. Fluffy. Bunny," replied Joey.

"What's that?" Violet asked.

"Do you live under a rock or something, Violet?" interjected Brian.

"Don't worry, Violet. We'll show you," said Tommy.

Lucy and Mark came inside to get the group. They told them that everything was ready to go outside and encouraged them to enjoy themselves, though without being too loud because the neighbors were trying to sleep. Violet was about to ask them if they had the items to make s'mores, but before she could get the question out Lucy walked right out with everything they needed. She also added that they had a collection of sticks to use as pokers so they could roast the marshmallows. The kids were having their first campout of the summer and were determined to make it the best one yet. Lucy and Mark again told them to have fun and that they were going to go get some sleep and see them in the morning. All the kids waved, expressed their gratitude, and said it was nice to meet Violet's parents.

Before Lucy and Mark went to bed, they relaxed and had a conversation of their own.

"Do you think she knows?" asked Mark.

"I don't think she suspects a thing," replied Lucy.

"Oh come on! She has to know who we are by now" said Mark. "You don't think it was suspicious that we know so much about her?"

"Have you ever heard the term 'mothers know best'?"

"I just think you possibly gave too much away by ordering her favorite food and drink," said Mark. "You could've had her tell you the order."

"We made a promise that we would take care of her for the time being and make her feel as comfortable as possible."

"I get it. A promise is a promise."

"Let's get some sleep."

Meanwhile, in the backyard, the groups of kids were having the time of their lives, making s'mores, telling scary stories, having pillow fights, and making shadow puppets with a flashlight. Before they went to bed, they wanted to get in a game of chubby fluffy bunny. Violet was unfamiliar with the game, so Tommy took time to explain it to her. Violet really admired Tommy for this. All his patience and understanding made her feel really welcomed. Tommy explained the objective of the game: Each time you put a marshmallow in your mouth, you had to say "chubby fluffy bunny." Whoever got the most marshmallows in his or her mouth while still being able to say the phrase was the winner. Violet thought that this was the weirdest game she'd ever heard of, but why not? The worst that could happen was that she would have fun and get a good laugh out of it too.

"Everyone ready?" asked Tommy.

"Ready," the rest of the group replied.

They all stuck the first marshmallows in their mouths and didn't have a problem saying "chubby fluffy bunny." Then the next one and the next one—still no problem. Tommy suggested that they start sticking two marshmallows in their mouths at a time, and that's when things started getting harder. Pretty soon they were all drooling from the mouth and laughing at each other. Everyone looked so ridiculous with a mouth full of marshmallows, still trying to say "chubby fluffy bunny." Every word seemed to be coming out in slow motion. First Samantha dropped out, then Brian, then John, then Joey, and, finally, Melissa. The last two standing were Violet and Tommy. They were determined to keep going, but Tommy stuck out his hand and called for a truce. The game was over, and they couldn't help but continue to laugh at one another.

"You should've seen the look on our faces. Priceless," said Brian.

"I was worried that I was going to choke from laughing so hard, so I couldn't do it anymore," said Samantha.

"Same here," John offered.

"Better safe than sorry," added Melissa.

"Of course Tommy and Violet are the last ones out," said Joey. "Looks like you've finally found some competition, Tommy."

"You could be right," said Tommy.

"Hey, I noticed that everything is a competition with you guys. Why?" Violet asked.

"Friends are supposed to challenge each other. That's how we bring out the best in ourselves and make each other better, but the most important thing is to have fun," replied Tommy. "But hey, let's get some sleep. We can head over to my house early in the morning."

"This night was so much fun! I can't wait to make more memories this summer," Brian added.

"We should do this every week," said other members of the group.

Everyone headed into the tent and fell asleep right away except Violet and Tommy. Tommy expressed to Violet that she was one of the coolest kids he'd ever met and hoped they would stay friends forever. He made a promise that they would, but Violet hesitated to respond before saying, "Of course." Tommy asked Violet if everything was okay, and Violet said, "Yes. We should just get some sleep." She didn't fall asleep for quite some time though. She felt bad about having made a promise to Tommy that they would be friends forever and having agreed with the group that they'd do this every week. The idea that she couldn't stay here forever popped up again in her mind, but she also was wondering about when and how she would be able to go home.

Morning finally came, and it was time to head over to Tommy's. The group wanted to clean up first out of respect for Violet's parents. They were guests in their house, so the least they could do was clean up. After cleaning up, they all wanted to get breakfast, but Tommy told them not to worry about it because they could get breakfast at his house. Before they left, Violet wanted to head inside and tell Lucy and Mark that she was heading to Tommy's, but they weren't there. She checked the family room, the bedroom, and the kitchen. When Violet entered the kitchen, she noticed a folded piece of paper on the counter, so she walked over and opened it. The note said, "Gone for the day. You and your friends can help yourselves to some food if you'd all like. See you soon. Love, Lucy and Mark." Violet thought that it was odd that they would just leave like that, but she had a full day ahead of her, so off she went with Tommy and the gang.

As Violet rode over to Tommy's house, she realized that she would get to see her grandparents in this time. She had met her grandma in her other life, but never her grandpa, so she was pretty excited about that. Violet also was worried that her mom back home might be looking for her, so, again, sooner or later she would have to figure out a way to get home. Maybe another picture was the key, one that would suck her back into her room. She sure didn't want her mom to have to worry about her any more than she already was, especially after everything that had happened at school.

They arrived at Tommy's house, and there to greet them was Tommy's dog, Spunky. This dog really reminded her of Buster. Buster had died of old age, and Violet didn't know if she would get a dog ever again, so it was nice for her to be around one. Tommy's mom was there to greet them too. She was working in the garden—watering the flowers and picking vegetables from their garden. She looked really happy to see them, and right away Tommy introduced Violet to her. Tommy's mom said it was a pleasure to meet Violet and that there was breakfast inside if they wanted any. Everyone headed inside and took a seat at the kitchen table. Tommy's dad then walked into the room. He told them not to worry about getting breakfast and that it would be coming right up. He also wondered who the new girl was, so Tommy introduced Violet to his dad as well. Tommy's dad asked everyone if they liked their eggs sunny-side up or scrambled, and they all replied scrambled. No one was prepared for what was about to happen next, though.

As Tommy's dad was making scrambled eggs, he started staggering and eventually collapsed. Tommy ran over to him and told everyone else to run outside and tell his mom to call 911. Tommy kept shaking his dad, but nothing happened. He kept pleading for his dad to wake up, but still nothing. Tommy's mom rushed in and told Tommy to leave, that the paramedics, who were on their way, had said to not touch his stricken father. Everyone was in shock because this had come out of nowhere. They were about to have a nice breakfast and then have another full day of fun, but tragedy had gotten in the way.

The paramedics came in and started performing CPR, but it had no effect, so they put Tommy's dad on a stretcher and said that only family could ride in the back. Tommy told them not to worry and just to meet him at the hospital. Finally, the ambulance took off, and the kids ran to their bikes, got on, and tried to keep up. It was no use; the ambulance was going too fast. They still stayed the route to the hospital because they knew that Tommy needed them at this moment. They arrived at the hospital fifteen minutes later and quickly got off their bikes and headed inside. Once inside the hospital, they ran toward the front desk and asked where Tommy and his parents were.

The lady at the front desk said they were in the ICU and Tommy's dad was breathing once again but hadn't woken up yet. Violet and everyone else headed to the ICU on the third floor and found the room that Tommy's dad was in. They saw Tommy and his mom sitting in the waiting room, hugging each other, and decided to join in. Tommy's mom then mentioned that there was a room for prayer and they should turn to God during this time. She said that the group of kids were more than welcome to join them. Violet didn't know how to feel about this, but she decided to be there for Tommy. During prayer, though, she had a change of heart and became angry.

"How can you turn to God during a time like this?"

"God is love. He provides when one is in need," replied Tommy's mom.

"God will heal my father and get us through this rough time," added Tommy.

"Okay, if God loves us so much, then why would this happen?" asked Violet. "God's not real. This is all something you tell yourselves to feel better."

In that moment Violet had enough of all this and ran out of the room. Tommy wanted to run after Violet, but his mom held him back. She explained to Tommy that some aren't ready to accept and believe in God, but that it would all happen in

God's timing. Tommy was still sad, though, and still wanted to run after Violet. Selfless and kind, Tommy was willing to set aside his problems and be there for Violet but wanted to stay and be there for his mom too. He took his mom's advice and decided to stay with her.

Violet had made her way into the hall and kept running and running. She made her way to the stairs and rushed down to get out of the hospital as soon as possible. Violet couldn't understand why people turned to something that she considered a fairytale. It seemed like a huge waste of time to her, and she felt she couldn't be a part of it. Violet made her way outside, hopped on Tommy's bike, and started riding toward Lucy and Mark's house. When she arrived, she made her way to the door. As she opened it to go inside and see if Lucy and Mark were home, she was blinded by a flash of light.

Four

Violet's first journey with her dad was over. She didn't want it to be over because she'd had so much fun with him and his friends. Violet wanted to live in that moment forever, but that wasn't the reality of life. Violet was going to have to face what was going on in her life and there was no escaping it. It was a new day and more adventures were waiting for her. There was also a pleasant surprise waiting for her at school. One that would be her first bit of hope.

Violet was all of a sudden back in her room in the Cooper family house and was sad at first because she didn't even get to say goodbye to Tommy. Her departure from the other time just happened out of nowhere, and she wished she could go back. Violet headed over to the picture she had of her dad when he was a kid, but nothing happened. She shook it and shook it, but still nothing. Violet thought to herself, *Why isn't this stupid thing working?* She then heard her name called over and over again and realized it was Mrs. Cooper looking for her. Violet hoped that her mom hadn't been looking for her too long, but she decided it was for the best to get to her and let her know that she was home and well. She made her way downstairs and followed the sound of her mom's voice.

"Violet…Violet…where are you?"

"Mom, don't worry. I'm coming. Be right there."

"Violet, you had me worried sick. I couldn't find you. Anyway, go and get ready for school," said Violet's mom. "Also, remember you have to see Mrs. Turner first thing in the morning for your session."

Violet then hurriedly got ready for school. As she was getting ready, she thought about her time with Tommy and his friends, about how fun it had been. Violet didn't want to go to school because that was a place where she didn't have that type of thing—friends, that is. Violet got dressed, put her things in her backpack, and just like the other morning, she looked at herself in the mirror to prep herself for going back to school. Another memory of her time with Tommy showed up in her mind, and she remembered what he had said: "You don't have to do everything alone. Friends are there if you want them to be."

Violet heard her mom call her again and told her to hurry, that she'd be waiting in the car for her. Violet then grabbed everything she needed for the day and met her mom in the car. It was pretty quiet at first on the way to school, but Violet's mom decided to break the silence. She asked Violet how she was doing, and Violet replied that she was doing okay but was kind of tired, so she didn't really feel like talking. Her mom asked if she was having trouble sleeping; Violet knew the real reason she was tired but couldn't tell her mom. She decided to tell her that she had a lot on her mind lately ever since the events of yesterday, and that this was getting in the way of sleep. Violet's mom was worried that Violet would have another rough day at school and hoped that Mrs. Turner could turn things around. She hated the idea of getting another call from the principal.

They arrived at the school, and Violet didn't even bother to say goodbye to her mom. She quickly got out of the car and made her way to the door. As she was passing other students, she noticed a girl sitting on a wooden bench by herself. Violet had never seen this girl at school before. She also noticed how sad the girl looked. *Is this girl new?* thought Violet. If she was, she was probably scared of her first day at a new school. Violet didn't bother to stop and moved on.

Mrs. Summers was standing there ready to meet her kids, just like every other morning. She was especially happy to see Violet because she wasn't certain her pupil would show up after what had happened yesterday. Mrs. Summers wanted to know how Violet had been doing since then.

"Hey, Violet! How are you feeling today?"

"Hi," responded Violet.

Mrs. Summers was pretty down that Violet didn't really respond to her but was also pretty content with getting a hi, seeing as Violet didn't usually greet anyone in the morning. She would always walk in with her head down, not say a word, and just take a seat at her desk. That was the thing, though— Violet had also walked in with her head up this morning, so Mrs. Summers could only hope that things would be different from here on out. One could only hope.

Violet put her stuff away, got everything out that she need-ed for the day, and headed to her desk. As soon as Violet took a seat, she got out a piece of paper and crayons. This caught Mrs. Summers's attention because normally when Violet sat down, she would just lay her head on her desk until it was time to start the school day. Mrs. Summers was curious and decided to go over and see what Violet was drawing. Violet saw what she was trying to do but wouldn't let her see because she was a private person. Mrs. Summers didn't take it personally and saw that it was time to greet the kids, just like every morning, so she headed toward the door. As Mrs. Summers was standing by the door, she kept wondering what Violet was drawing; even if she wouldn't show it to her, maybe she would show it to Mrs. Turner during today's session.

It was 9:00 a.m., and the school day had started, but before Mrs. Summers started the first subject of the day, she wanted to write something important on a sticky note to Mrs. Turner. Mrs. Summers went over to her desk, got out a sticky note and pen, and wrote, "Ask her about the picture she was drawing this morning." Mrs. Summers then folded it up, handed it to Violet, and sent her down to Mrs. Turner. Violet dreaded the idea of having to see Mrs. Turner every morning. Deep down inside, she didn't want to go, but also deep down inside, she had a feeling that this was the only way that things were going to get better so there was no escaping it.

Violet got to Mrs. Turner's office, and the door was shut, so she knocked. Mrs. Turner asked who it was, and to her surprise, it was Violet. Mrs. Turner was really happy to see her. She wasn't expecting Violet to come to school and was amazed that she had shown up. Violet walked up to her, handed her the note that Mrs. Summers had written, and took a seat. Mrs. Turner started with small talk, asking how she was doing, and Violet responded with "Okay, I guess." Then she went silent. Mrs. Turner looked at the note and decided that it was time to get started; there was no time to waste because they only had forty-five minutes together per day.

"Violet, first off I am glad to see you today, and I'm also glad that today is the first day of finding ways to move forward and cope with your situation. But it all starts with you," said Mrs. Turner.

"What does that mean?"

"I can't help you if you don't tell me what's going on inside that noggin of yours. I'm not a mind reader," replied Mrs. Turner. "How about we start off with the note that Mrs. Summers gave me. Sound good?"

Violet didn't say anything but only nodded.

"Tell me about the drawing you made this morning."

Violet again didn't speak. She took a piece of paper out of her pocket and slid it over to Mrs. Summers.

"This is pretty good. There's—I'm guessing—you in the middle, but who are these other kids? There are four boys and two girls."

"That's my dad when he was younger and his friends, Brian, Joey, John, Melissa, and Samantha."

"Why did you choose this particular scene?"

"Well, I found this shoebox in the attic and found all this cool stuff my dad must've collected over the years. Then I got sucked into the picture and..." Violet realized that her excitement about the adventure had caused her to speak more than she should have, and so she immediately stopped.

"You got sucked into a picture? Hmm. You must be writing a story and making pictures along with it. Am I right?"

Violet then saw an opportunity to go along with Mrs. Turner, so her secret wouldn't be found out.

"Yeah, a story," she replied.

"Could you tell me more about this story?"

"Sure. We played at the beach and went on adventures, and it was so much fun!"

"How does making these stories make you feel?"

"Relaxed, happy, and relieved."

"You know, Violet, I think this could be very good for you. Personally, I think you should continue."

Before Mrs. Turner could say anything else, she looked at the clock and saw that it was time for Violet to head back to class. She was overall happy with how things had gone. Violet usually never talked during these sessions, and there would be a good amount of awkward silence, but she had talked today. Even though Violet wasn't actually writing a story, Mrs. Turner thought that Violet had found a way to deal with what was going on. Maybe, as time went on, she would start opening up more about the underlying issues, but only time would tell. Mrs. Turner then asked if Violet would like to join her for lunch. Violet's response shocked her and made Mrs. Turner feel even better about how things were starting to go.

"Violet, would you like to join me for lunch again? I know you don't really like to eat in the cafeteria or go to recess, so the offer is there."

"Not today, Mrs. Turner. I think I may go find a friend to eat and play with during recess."

"Wow, why the sudden change? The reason I ask is because it seemed like for the longest time, you had trouble stepping outside of the box and putting yourself out there."

"Just some advice I heard from someone I met the other day. That's all."

As Violet was about to leave, she turned to Mrs. Turner for some advice. This shocked Mrs. Turner even more.

"Mrs. Turner, why is it that I've had trouble for quite some time making friends and getting close to others?"

"When you deal with a great loss, especially of someone who was once a big part of your life and is now gone, you put your guard up so it will never happen again."

"How do I take that guard down?"

"It will take time, Violet, but what I would say is, whatever advice you heard, take it and go with it."

"How do I make friends?"

"Just be yourself. I don't know if you know this or not, but you have a lot to offer, Violet. You just have to look inside yourself and see it."

Violet then thanked Mrs. Turner and left. Once again, Mrs. Turner was ecstatic about what had just happened. Violet had finally opened up about something she'd been having trouble with. Mrs. Turner knew this was a huge step for her. *The story must be helping her open up more in these sessions*, thought Mrs. Turner. Whatever it was, she wasn't going to question it, and she was grateful for the progress that had been made today. Mrs. Turner then thought it would be a good idea to call Violet's mom right away and tell her the good news.

"Mrs. Cooper, this is the school psychologist, Mrs. Turner. How are you?"

"I'm doing well," replied Mrs. Cooper. "I'm going to assume this is about Violet, right? How did her first session go?"

"It went well, actually."

"How so?"

"It seems that Violet found this shoebox in your home, and it has all these pictures and items your husband collected over the years. Violet tells me that she's making a story about it, and it seems to be helping."

"Shoebox? This is something new to me," said Mrs. Cooper. "How will this help her out? Is this even healthy?"

"It sounds like she's writing a story about his life and has included herself in it. Seems to me that this will be an adventure they go on. You know, I've had children in the past who have created stories that helped them deal with great loss. This could be the answer that helps Violet reach the conclusion that we've been trying to help her reach."

"She opened up to you today?" Mrs. Cooper asked with shock in her voice.

"Yes, she asked me if I would give her some advice—she told me that she wanted to try to make friends today and didn't know how to," replied Mrs. Turner. "She also wanted to know why she's been having so much trouble trying."

"So we continue to let her write and go from there?"

"Most certainly. And, again, don't go to her about this, let her come to you. These stories are always really private, and feelings are put into them as well."

"Thank you, and will do. Talk with you soon."

As Violet was walking back to class, she was able to peer into one of the classrooms and noticed the same girl she had seen sitting on the bench earlier. The rest of the class was at the carpet with the teacher, but this girl remained at her seat. She had the same sad look on her face, and Violet could only speculate about what was going through her mind. Violet felt bad for her; she could relate to the girl's feelings. Violet knew that look and feeling all too well.

Violet arrived back at class, and it was time for math. The class was going to work on multiplication tables today, and Mrs. Summers asked the class to come to the carpet for the lesson. Mrs. Summers saw that Violet was getting all her things for math and joining them at the carpet. This made Mrs. Summers quite happy, and she became more energetic because Violet hadn't joined them for quite a while. Mrs. Summers had some hope that things were starting to go in the right direction for Violet. She didn't participate when she was called on or when it was time to work in pairs, but Mrs. Summers took whatever she could get out of her.

The morning went by quite fast; soon it was time for lunch. Just as Mrs. Turner had, Mrs. Summers asked Violet if she would like to eat lunch with her and stay inside for recess. Again Violet said that she was going to try something different today. Mrs. Summers didn't say much, but she was smiling brightly on the inside. She told Violet that she had appreciated her joining them at the carpet today and at least trying to participate. Violet didn't say anything to her, only smiled and headed off to lunch.

Violet walked into the cafeteria and looked around for a place to sit. There was that girl again, sitting alone. It didn't look like anyone was trying to join her. For one split second, Violet was about to move on and find some other people to sit with, but that same light she'd been seeing shone through the window onto the girl. At that moment, Violet knew this could possibly be the friend she was supposed to make today, so she went over to sit with the lonely-looking girl.

"You mind if I sit with you?"

"Not at all. Feel free."

"My name's Violet. It's nice to meet you."

"My name's Isabella Evans, and it's nice to meet you too."

"Haven't seen you around here, so I'm guessing you're new."

"You guessed right. This is my sixth time moving in four years."

"The sixth time! Why so much?"

"My father's a pastor, so he gets relocated a lot."

"That's got to be hard."

"It can be. You never get a chance to make real friends, so I'm hoping that this is the last move for quite some time."

"Hey, after lunch would you like to play with me out on the playground?"

"I would love to."

Violet had put herself out there, and it seemed like it was going to pay off. They had a good time at lunch and found out they had a lot in common. They had the same favorite movies, foods, candy, and even the same favorite school subject. This felt like a match made in heaven for Violet. One thing she was iffy about, though, was Isabella being a pastor's kid, which meant that she had been brought up in a household that believed in God. Violet was afraid that if Isabella found out about how she felt about God, she would reconsider their friendship, so she just kept that to herself. She could only hope that Isabella wouldn't ever bring up God.

It was time to go out to recess, and Violet asked Isabella what she wanted to play. Isabella looked around and saw all the possibilities. There was the playscape, hopscotch, jump rope, hula hoop, and the swings. The playground was theirs for the taking, so Isabella just took off and told Violet to follow her.

Isabella made her way to the playscape and raced up the ladder, teasing Violet that she should try to keep up. They raced up the ladder, ran across the bridge in the middle, went across the monkey bars, and zoomed down the slide. Isabella asked Violet if she was tired yet, and Violet responded, "No way. Let's keep going." They raced up and down the playscape several times and then moved to the swings. Isabella challenged Violet to a contest of who could go higher. All these challenges reminded Violet of her time with her dad and his friends; she had a feeling that Isabella was going to be a friend who could make her better and bring out the best in her. After they were done with the swings, Isabella and Violet were all tired out, so they decided to go lie down in the grass and talked until it was time to go in.

"The sky is so beautiful," said Violet.

"It's like God put it there just for us. I'm always amazed by his creations," Isabella responded.

Violet's hope that Isabella wouldn't bring up God came to an end quite quickly, so she shifted the conversation in another direction.

"So, Isabella, math is your favorite subject too?"

"Yeah, there's something about putting numbers together that I really like."

"It's like you have pieces of a puzzle, and you're trying to put the puzzle back together."

"Wow, I've never heard that one before, but it sounds pretty accurate," said Isabella. "Hey, we should have a hangout at my place sometime and work on math homework together. It would be so much fun!"

"I think I'll be busy in the coming weeks, but I'll let you know."

The bell had rung, and recess was over. Before the new friends parted ways for the rest of the day, Isabella told Violet that she had a lot of fun and hoped that they could eat lunch together and play during recess again tomorrow. Violet said that she had a lot of fun, too, and was looking forward to tomorrow. Violet was still thinking about the offer that Isabella made about coming over to do homework sometime. Even though it sounded like a lot of fun, she was leaning toward declining the invite. Violet was again afraid of the idea of hanging out at the house of a pastor's kid. What would Isabella and her parents think if they found out that Violet didn't believe in God? They would possibly try to talk with her to change her stance on God. Violet remembered how angry she got every time her mom brought up God and didn't want to feel the same way toward Isabella. It could possibly ruin their friendship. Violet already felt like she was ruining the friendship by not being honest with Isabella. She was afraid of being judged, but she was judging Isabella because she was assuming that if Isabella knew the truth, she might not fully accept her.

On the way back to class, Violet passed Isabella's classroom. Isabella saw her, smiled, and waved, but Violet acted like she didn't notice and kept on going. When Violet arrived at class, Mrs. Summers asked Violet how things were going, and Violet told her that she had made a new friend named Isabella. Mrs. Summers knew Isabella was the new girl and thought it was awfully nice of Violet to gravitate toward her and make her feel welcomed. It's always nice to make a new friend on your first day at a new school. Mrs. Summers then asked the class to join her at the carpet for story time. Mrs. Summers was going to read them a Dr. Seuss book. Violet felt like her heart had dropped into her stomach when she heard that but got up and joined them at the carpet anyways.

As Mrs. Summers read on, she noticed Violet was acting strange. Violet couldn't sit still and kept looking at the clock, the same thing she'd been doing the other day. Mrs. Summers couldn't put the pieces together until she noticed that Violet only started acting strange when story time involved a Dr. Seuss book. She was going to go with her gut feeling that this was the reason and thought it would be nice if Mrs. Turner addressed the issue with Violet. Mrs. Summers looked again at Violet and saw that her state of agitation was getting worse, so she asked Violet if she'd like to leave and take a walk. Violet gave a sigh of relief and headed out the door. As Violet was walking down the hallway, Isabella spotted her and noticed that something wasn't right with her friend. She asked to leave the classroom so she could check on Violet.

"Violet, are you all right?"

"Not right now."

"You don't look so good."

"*Not right now! I need you to leave me alone!*" Violet had a stern look on her face and agitation in her voice.

"Jeez, sorry for trying to help. I'll leave you be, though," Isabella said with a somber voice.

Violet felt bad about what she had done. Isabella was just trying to help, and she had driven her away, just as she had so many others. She really wanted to open up and accept people's help, but she couldn't. Something was holding her back, but she didn't know what that was. Violet was also upset at herself for acting this way over a book. It was a book that brought joy to all kids who read it, and yet she didn't want anything to do with it.

Violet's next journey though would make her realize what she was missing. It would show her a quality deep inside that she never knew she had. A certain someone was going to show her the way and bring this quality to the surface.

Violet headed back to class and tried to calm down with her cassette player, but it only did so much this time. This episode had caused Violet to take a couple of steps back. She was out of it for the rest of the day. She was really happy when she came back from recess, yet all it had taken was one moment to throw her day off. Mrs. Summers knew there had to be something significant about the Dr. Seuss book that triggered Violet. She wasn't going to look more into it though; she was going to leave that up to Mrs. Turner. Mrs. Summers was still happy with Violet's progress today and had high hopes for her moving forward.

It was time to go home. Violet quickly got her stuff and made her way to the school parking lot where her mom was waiting for her in the car. Violet was anxious about getting back to the shoebox to see what else was in there. She wanted a way to see her dad again but was worried that she wouldn't be able to because when she had tried to go back into the picture that morning, it wouldn't let her.

There has to be another way to see him, but how? thought Violet. She knew there was something special about the shoebox but couldn't quite wrap her mind around it. Violet then remembered that she had briefly noticed a picture of her mom, her dad, and her on her fourth birthday. Violet came up with a crazy idea.

If I was able to see my dad as a kid, then I can also see him at the time of my fourth birthday. That way I can stop him from leaving and everything will change. We can be a family again, thought Violet. Violet got in the car and told her mom that they needed to get home as soon as possible. On the way home, Violet realized that she couldn't try to go on another journey in the middle of the day. Her mom would end up noticing that she was gone. Violet told herself that she would wait until it was time for bed—that would be her chance to sneak up to the attic. Her mom would be asleep, so she wouldn't suspect a thing.

"Mom, you don't have to hurry anymore. It's okay," Violet said.

"What was the hurry anyway?" her mom asked.

"I'm just really hungry, but food can wait. Rather be safe anyway. Wouldn't want you to get into an accident."

"I appreciate your concern about my safety. I'll make dinner as soon as we get home," said Violet's mom. "Also, I heard some good news today from Mrs. Turner. Would you like to talk about it at dinner tonight?"

"Sure..." Violet replied with uncertainty in her voice.

Violet's mom heard some uncertainty in that response, but it was better than nothing. She thought she should be careful and not push too much when they eventually talked. At the last moment, though, Jennifer had a change of plans. She wanted to bond with her daughter before dinner and she knew exactly what to do.

"Change of plans, Violet. How about before we go home and have dinner, we stop and get some ice cream? I know just the place where we can enjoy our ice cream too."

"You're going to let me have ice cream before dinner?"

"A little ice cream before dinner won't hurt you."

"What about our talk?"

"We can still talk at dinner, but let's go have some fun."

"Yeah, I would like that a lot."

Jennifer was thrilled that Violet agreed to getting ice cream together. This was her first chance to bond and to try to get their relationship back to what it used to be. She knew that ice cream came second to Violet's favorite dessert, strawberry waffles with whip cream, so she had a feeling that it was going to be hard for her to turn down. Jennifer's surprise place to take Violet was Friendship Park. This was the park that Jennifer, her late husband Tommy, and Violet had gone to every Sunday after church for an afternoon of fun. They would have a family picnic under a giant oak tree, catch butterflies, and take long walks on the park's path. Jennifer and Tommy also sat on a park bench to enjoy the view as well as watching their daughter have a good time.

Jennifer wanted to take Violet to places where she had good memories and wanted to create more. This was one of Violet's favorite parks when she was younger. Mrs. Cooper had only the best intentions when she had planned this, but she didn't know about the episode that Violet had earlier that day.

Once Violet and her mom got their ice cream; they got back in the car to head to Friendship Park. As they got closer to the destination, Jennifer told Violet to keep her eyes shut until they arrived, because it was a surprise. Mrs. Cooper couldn't wait to see the look on Violet's face once she realized where they were. She was expecting Violet to be excited, but she was in for an unpleasant surprise.

"Ok, sweetie, you can open. Look where we are."

Violet opened her eyes and felt the same anxious feeling when Mrs. Summers had announced to the class that she was going to read them Dr. Seuss. She didn't want to be a part of anything that reminded her of the trauma she endured when her father died. This time Violet didn't have anywhere to go. She was inside a moving car. She felt trapped, and this only made her anxiety worse.

"Let me out! Let me out!" yelled Violet as she kept yanking the car door handle.

"What's wrong? You love this place."

"I don't want to be here. Please don't make me go."

"It's a gorgeous day, Violet. I thought it would be nice to sit outside and enjoy some ice cream."

"I'm not getting out. You can't make me."

Jennifer thought to herself as to why Violet didn't want to be at Friendship Park and then it hit her; Violet didn't want anything to do with the memories that her and her dad created there. Bringing Violet to a place that reminded her of her father was another trigger. Jennifer was beside herself with sadness when she realized what she'd just done.

"Ok, Violet. We can go some other place if you'd like or we can go home."

"Could we just go home? I'm not in the mood for ice cream anymore."

"Sure thing, kiddo."

Jennifer was filled with disappointment because the opportunity to spend more time with her daughter was over before it even started. She wasn't the only one disappointed, though. Violet glanced over at her mom and saw the long look on her face. She felt really bad because she knew deep down inside that her mom had been really looking forward to this and felt responsible for ruining it. What bothered Violet the most about moments like these is that it made her feel different. All the other kids at her school seemed normal to her, and she felt like the complete opposite.

"Mom, is there something wrong with me?"

"What made you ask this?"

"I just don't feel like I'm growing like the other kids at school. They live normal lives and I don't."

"Don't say that about yourself, sweetie. Let me tell you the story about the four flowers:

"Once upon a time, there was a farmer who planted four flowers in his garden. Over time, the flowers grew, but they didn't blossom at the same time. The first flower that blossomed felt proud and looked down on all the others that were still growing. Eventually the second and third flowers blossomed and started arguing with each other on who was more special. Finally the fourth flower blossomed, and all the other flowers started poking fun because it was the last to grow.

"All the other flowers would make comments like "You don't belong in the same garden as us" and "You'll be forgotten while the rest of us will be picked and end up on display in a home." This made the fourth flower feel rejected, until one day he saw all the other flowers again arguing with each other on who was the greatest. For the first time, this made the fourth flower notice something that it wished it'd seen before. Even though they all grew, one after the other, each one ended up the same: a big, beautiful flower. It no longer mattered to the fourth one that it grew last.

"See, Violet, it doesn't matter if you're taking longer than the other kids to grow into who you're supposed to be."

"Wow, I never looked at it that way."

"Stop worrying so much. Just like the fourth flower, you're going to blossom into something beautiful one day. Your support group and I believe in you."

"Thanks, Mom. I feel a lot better now."

This was a very touching moment between Jennifer and her daughter. Jennifer was extremely happy that she was able to turn Violet's frown into a smile. She loved Violet and wanted nothing but the best for her. Jennifer could only hope and pray that Violet molded into who she was truly supposed to be.

When they got home, Violet rushed to her room, having told her mom that she needed some time to herself for a while. Once Violet got into her room, she put on her cassette player again, lay on her bed, and thought about what had happened with the Dr. Seuss book and at the park. She was still upset about it, but as usual she ignored her emotions and thoughts. Violet thought some rest would make her feel better, and when she rolled over on her bed, she was facing toward her bookshelf. A Dr. Seuss book caught her eye. The book had never been there before, and Violet began to wonder how it had gotten there. Violet decided to turn the other way and tried to get some rest before dinner. Yet no matter how hard she tried to ignore her thoughts, she couldn't. She was trying to suppress a memory, but if she continued to do so, her emotions would continue to come out in the worst ways, just like they had to-day. She was going to have to come to terms with her feelings someway, somehow.

After Violet tried to get a few more minutes of rest, her mom called her to dinner. Violet grabbed a plate, took a seat, and told her Mom about her new friend that she made at school today.

"I made a new friend today."

"That's great! Why don't you tell me a little bit about your new friend?"

"Her name's Isabella Evans, she's moved quite a lot, and her dad's a pastor."

"She's a pastor's kid. How wonderful."

"I had a feeling you'd be excited about that."

"What? Pastor's kids usually come from good homes. She could be a good influence on you."

"Anyway, we really connected today. We found out that we actually have a lot in common," replied Violet. "But some-thing happened at school today with her, and I'm afraid that I ruined our friendship just like that."

"Can you tell me what happened? Maybe I can help."

"Well, you know how I feel about God, so when I found out that she was a pastor's kid, I was already trying to distance myself from her. I was afraid that she would think differently about me if she knew how I felt about God and decide to no longer be my friend. I was already thinking about giving up."

"You don't know that. You can't assume things like that, Violet. You're judging her by thinking that she's going to judge you for your beliefs. That doesn't sound too fair to me."

"What if she doesn't want to be my friend after she finds out?"

"There you go again. You're judging," Mrs. Cooper interjected. "Let me ask you this: I know how you feel about God, but do you think I look at you any differently?"

"No, but you're my mom."

"That's not the point. The point is she'll accept you no matter what if she's truly a follower of God. Plus, like I said, she could be a good influence on you."

"There's one more thing, though."

"Go on."

"I'm not ready to tell her about my situation, and I don't want her to find out."

"It's always important to be honest and open with friends. That's how you make and keep them," offered Violet's mom. "Tell her when you're ready. When you feel the time is right."

Violet finished dinner, and her mom told her to not worry about cleaning up her plate; Violet had had a long day, and her mom wanted her to go get some rest. As Violet was walking away, she turned back to her mom and said, "Thanks today for everything. Love you."

"You're welcome, and love you too," her mom replied. She proceeded to clean up the table and wash the dishes. Just like Mrs. Summers and Mrs. Turner, Violet's mom was really happy with the progress that Violet was making. She felt like she was getting her daughter back and thought to herself, *God, whatever you're doing, I hope it continues to work.*

Violet went back into her bedroom, got ready for bed, and lay back down. She wanted to get back to the shoebox to carry out her plan, but she needed to wait till her mom went to bed, so she needed something to do to pass the time. Violet remembered that Mrs. Turner thought she was actually writing a story and thought it would be cool if she actually wrote about the adventure she had had with her dad. She went over to her bookshelf, grabbed a notebook and pencil, and started writing. She wanted to include pictures as well, so she went back to the bookshelf to grab some crayons. As she was heading to the bookshelf a second time, she noticed the Dr. Seuss book again. Violet was tired of it and didn't want to look at it any longer, so she put the book under her bed.

Several hours had passed. Violet heard her mom going up the stairs and heading to her room to go to sleep. It sounded like her mom was coming to Violet's room first, though, so she rushed to put everything away, turned off the lights, and jumped in bed to make it look as though she were sleeping. Her mom peeked in for a moment to check on Violet and proceeded to head to her own room. This was Violet's chance to head to the attic and get back to the shoebox. The floors squeaked with every step, so she was going to have to move quietly. Violet made her way to the door, opened it, and looked toward her mom's room to confirm that the lights were off. She continued to tiptoe all the way to the stairs that led up to the attic.

Violet was finally in the clear and ran up the stairs toward the dresser. There was the shoebox, right where she had left it. Violet opened the shoebox and rummaged through it, searching for the photo of her on her fourth birthday. It was sitting all the way at the bottom of the shoebox. Violet thought that this was going to be it. She was going to go in there and save her dad. This was the answer to all her problems. Violet remembered that a tear had done the trick in the case of the last picture, so she made herself cry a little. A couple of teardrops fell on the picture and—nothing. Violet started getting frustrated that this wasn't working and threw the shoebox across the room. She couldn't believe that she wasn't going to be able to carry out her plan and fell to the ground in agony.

Violet decided that it was pointless to stay up here, so she headed over to pick up the shoebox and put it away. As she went to pick it up, she noticed a newspaper article entitled "Hometown Hero." Violet read a little bit of the article and saw that it was about her father. She put the shoebox away and took the newspaper article with her, heading to her room. Again she had to be quiet so as not to wake up her mom. When Violet finally got to her room, she wanted to read the article, but suddenly she started feeling sleepy. She fell backward onto her bed, but she didn't exactly land on it. She just kept falling, falling, falling.

Five

Violet woke up. She felt like she had taken a fall, and her back was in pain. She felt around her; the surface on which she was lying was really cold, like marble. She looked up to find ceiling tiles. Violet was no longer in her room. So where was she? She sat up and started looking around to get an idea of her surroundings. Still Violet couldn't tell where she was. The building she was in had long hallways with dark blue lockers on each side; there were stairs that led to an upper level of the building and hundreds of doors that led to different rooms.

This place is huge. It would be so easy to get lost around here, thought Violet. Violet then noticed a girl standing to the right of her. She looked older, like a teenager, and was quite tall. The girl asked Violet if she was okay, and Violet asked her where she was. The girl was concerned, seeing that Violet had taken a hard fall. She then told Violet that she was at Bentley High and she'd better hurry up because she was going to miss the pep rally.

Violet thought to herself, *Bentley High? Pep rally?* The girl was still concerned and asked Violet if she was sure that she was okay. Violet responded yes, and the girl helped her up. When Violet stood up, she noticed that she was the same height as the girl. This freaked Violet out even more, and so she took off to find the closest mirror. The girl's locker was open, and a mirror hung on the door. Violet pushed the girl out of the way, stood before the mirror, and couldn't believe what she was seeing. Violet looked ten years older, and she was a lot taller too. She asked the girl more about the pep rally.

"So why are we going to this pep rally?"

"The Bentley High Cougars are taking on the Xavier High Falcons. Duh."

Violet decided to play along. "Right, of course. Sorry, I guess you were right about the fall. It made my memory a little foggy."

"It's going to be a good game. The winner gets a spot in the state championship game," the girl commented. "You sure you're okay? I can take you to the nurse's office if you want."

"No, I'm positive I'll be fine. How long till the pep rally?"

"It starts in about ten minutes."

Out of all the places Violet could've ended up! She had never even heard of this high school. And her appearance had changed so that she now resembled a teenage girl. The last thing she remembered was she suddenly felt tired, which caused her to fall backward on her bed, and now she was at Bentley High School.

This could be interesting, thought Violet. What was she going to learn this time? There had to be a reason she was here. Violet was done questioning things and decided that she was going to go with the flow. *I better get to that pep rally*. She didn't know what a pep rally was, but judging by the excitement of that girl, she had an idea that it was going to be fun, so she made her way to the gym.

Violet walked into the gym and was amazed at what she saw. There were so many students packed into this gym. She had never seen so many students in one place before. The most she'd ever been in a room with was thirty, but this was different. There had to be five hundred students in this gym. Violet saw that all the students were filling the bleachers, so she thought she better get a seat quickly. She looked around; there were cheerleaders and students holding signs—it was just so loud. The football coach approached the stage, and everyone went silent. The pep rally was finally starting.

"Ladies and gentlemen, we thank you for all your support throughout this season. We are thankful for each and every single one of you and couldn't have gotten this far without your support," said Coach Detmer. "Let's hear it for our Bentley High Cougars."

The crowd let out a big roar as the football team came out. There was one name that a lot of the students in the crowd were cheering for, and it caught Violet's attention.

"Tommy! Tommy! Tommy!" the crowd was yelling.

Tommy. . .that's my dad's name, thought Violet. She looked for him but couldn't pick him out among the football players. *My dad must look a lot different. He has aged as well since the last time I saw him, so it makes sense,* thought Violet. Since so many students were cheering him on, maybe he'd get up there and talk like the coach did. Violet was right. Not even a minute later, the coach introduced him.

"Now that the whole football team is out here, give a big round of applause for our team captain and star quarterback: Tommy Cooper!" said Coach Detmer with enthusiasm in his voice.

The crowd let out a big roar again and went silent as soon as Tommy grabbed the microphone from Coach Detmer.

"Make some noise!" shouted Tommy. The crowd let out another roar. "I can't hear you, Bentley High!" The crowd let out an even louder roar. "When I was given the opportunity to take over as the starting quarterback in my junior year, I made a promise to this school that we were going to bring home a title before I left. We came up short last year, but not this time. Two more games, and the title is ours!"

"We love you, Tommy," said a couple of students in the crowd.

"I love you all too. But bring this energy to the game tonight. We're going to need your support more than ever. Thank you, and *go Cougars!*"

The crowd stood up and applauded Tommy. They started chanting "Cougars! Cougars! Cougars!"

Wow! My dad. . .the star quarterback, thought Violet.

A couple more players took the stage to talk about how special the season had been to them and thanked all the fans. The last person to speak was Coach Detmer, who thanked the fans as well and encouraged them to show up for the game that night. The pep rally was over, and it was now time for the students to head back to class.

Wow! My dad, the star quarterback, Violet repeated to herself as she made her way down the bleachers. *Looks like I'm going to my first football game ever! This will be fun!* Violet walked out of the gym into the hallway and was clueless about where to go at that point. All the students were going back to their classrooms, but she had no idea where hers was, so she wandered the hallways for a while.

As she was walking through the hallways, she kept marveling at how big this school was. This place was like a castle compared to the elementary school she attended.

So many classrooms to choose from, but which one? thought Violet. She then got the idea to look for the classroom that her father was in. This could take a while, but she was willing to be patient if she could find her dad again. Before she could start the search, a man in a suit approached her; she had a feeling it was the principal of the school. Violet thought she was going to get in trouble for not being in class, but to her surprise, she was actually going to get a little help.

"Where are you supposed to be right now?" asked the principal.

"In...class?" replied Violet.

"Bingo. Now get to it."

"I'm kind of new, so I'm lost right now."

"Do you have your schedule on you? Every student is issued one."

"Not sure. Let me check."

Violet then started rummaging through her pockets. She felt a folded piece of paper and pulled it out.

"Here it is. Hmm...It says I'm supposed to be in environmental science in room 210."

"There you go. I'm going to the faculty lounge, and I better not see you out of class once I get back."

Phew, that was a close one, thought Violet. She didn't know where room 210 was, so she had to look around a little more; she knew she had to find it before the principal came back. Luckily there were signs before entering each hallway that could point her in the right direction. Violet read the signs, saying to herself, *100–150…No…151–190…No…Here it is! 191–210. Upstairs in the science wing.* She wasn't too fond of science (it was one of her least favorite subjects), but having a place to go for the time being was better than having no place to go. She couldn't just wander the hallways for the rest of the day. Violet made her way to the science wing on the second level, got to her classroom, and was greeted by the teacher.

"You're late," said the teacher.

Violet apologized, but the teacher still asked her for a note from the office excusing her tardiness. Violet explained that she was new and wasn't familiar with the rules. The teacher let it slide, just this once, and told her to take a seat. As Violet went to sit down, she looked around for her dad, but he wasn't anywhere to be seen. *Great. Not only am I in the world's most boring class, but my dad's not here either. What else could go wrong?* thought Violet.

Not even a moment later, her dad walked in and was greeted graciously by the teacher. He didn't have to give an explanation as to why he was late and didn't have to show a note from the office.

"What the heck! Is he a king or something?" Violet said quietly to herself.

A girl sitting behind her heard what she said and replied, "Tommy is, in fact, a really big deal around here. After all, he's the star quarterback and has a lot of offers to play in college. It should be no surprise to anyone that he gets special treatment."

Violet couldn't help but roll her eyes. The teacher started class and told the students to get out their text books and turn to page seventy-five. The teacher began to read, but Violet didn't bother paying attention. She was too fixated on her father. She couldn't help but keep looking at him, and the next comment from the girl behind her really annoyed her.

"Checking out Tommy Cooper, I see."

What does that mean? thought Violet.

"He's so hot," added the girl.

What is she talking about? Does she mean like "warm"? thought Violet.

"All the girls want to be Tommy's girlfriend, so get in line."

The lightbulb clicked on, and Violet now knew what the girl was talking about. She became nauseated by the comment and decided to turn around to let the student know she meant business in what she was about to say.

"Believe me when I say this: that will never ever happen, and I mean ever," Violet exclaimed.

"Whatever you say."

If you only knew, thought Violet.

The teacher had noticed what was going on and decided to intervene. "Am I boring you two? It has come to my attention that your conversation is more important than what's going on up here."

"Sorry," replied Violet.

"First you come into my class late, and now you think you're too good to listen?"

Violet began to slowly sink into her chair. She wasn't used to a teacher like this and started to get embarrassed. What the teacher was about to say didn't make things any better. "How about you start reading? That way I'll know you're paying attention."

Violet looked down at her book to see where they had left off and couldn't help but notice all these hard words—chlorophyll, fermentation, orographic. Even though Violet had aged and looked different, she still had the mind of an eight-year-old. There was no way she could read all this. As if this day could get any worse.

Here goes nothing, Violet thought to herself and took a deep breath.

As she was about to start reading, she heard a student say, "Let me read instead."

She looked to see who had spoken; it was her dad. The teacher said "no" at first but gave in after Tommy repeatedly insisted.

Violet then turned to her dad and mouthed the words *thank you*.

About an hour later, class was over, and it was time to go home. Violet tried to catch up to her dad to talk with him more and express how thankful she was that he had saved her, but he was in a hurry. Violet understood that he had a big game to get ready for that night, so she would have to wait for the perfect opportunity to approach him. The game started at seven in the evening, but when Violet looked at the clock hanging on the wall, she noticed it was only three in the afternoon, so she had four hours to spare.

Violet had to think about how she was going to pass the time.

What's there to do around here? she asked herself. Violet decided she would start by heading outside and go from there. When she got outside, she started walking to a main road. A lot of the surroundings looked familiar to her. Then it hit her.

Violet was back in the town of Spindale, North Carolina, but at a different time. *I'll just head into town and hangout at the Old Town Diner until it's time to go to the game,* thought Violet.

Violet arrived at the diner and saw the exact same booth where she had sat with Lucy and Mark. It was open. This made her think of them, and she wondered if they were still here and lived in the same house. She thought about the note they had left before she ended up going back to her own time, and it made her believe that they had to be there.

See you soon, thought Violet. She got excited and wanted to pay them a visit. This would also give her a place to stay. Violet didn't know exactly how long she was going to be here, so it would be nice to have a place to stay if she needed one.

The waitress came to take her order. Violet again ordered strawberry waffles with whip cream on top. Even though she had that a lot, it reminded her of home, which gave her comfort. After she finished her meal, there were still two hours left before game time. Violet tried to get the waitress's attention, and when she came over, Violet asked if they had any coloring books and crayons. The waitress gave her a weird look because it was odd that a teenager would ask for something that was normally the domain of kids whose parents wanted to prevent them from getting antsy.

Maybe she's still a kid at heart, thought the waitress.

Violet was a kid all right, but it wasn't only at heart. *This should make things go by faster,* thought Violet.

Violet got so into her coloring that she had lost track of time. The waitress came over to Violet and told her that they were going to close up soon so they could head to the game as well but said she was more than welcome to come back afterward. This was the place where all the players would come to celebrate after they had won a game. Violet looked at the clock and saw it was ten minutes to 7:00 p.m., so she had to hurry.

She got outside and started running back toward the high school. At first, she didn't know exactly where the football field was but saw the stadium lights and could hear all the fans. Violet reached the stadium in time for kickoff, but ran into another problem, which was a long line to get into the game.

Great, now I'll definitely be late for the game, she said to herself. Violet had to come up with a plan. She saw the marching band heading in through the side gates and saw her opportunity. She rushed over and tried to blend in with the band. She got in the front of one of the band members, who tapped her on the shoulder and said, "What do you think you're doing?"

"Shut up!" said Violet as she elbowed the band member behind her. As soon as they got through the gate, Violet broke off from the marching band and headed for the sideline so she could have a better view of the game.

What Violet was now seeing made the pep rally look like nothing. There were cheerleaders, the marching band was playing, and the two teams were warming up. The lights were so bright, but she noticed that this made the scene look even cooler. There were also hundreds of fans on each side. What stuck out to Violet the most was the student section. They were going absolutely crazy. They had signs, a lot of their faces were painted, and there were some guys in the front with their shirts off. They each had a letter painted on their chest and had lined up in such a way that they spelled out the word "Cougars."

These people are insane, thought Violet.

A voice coming from the loudspeaker said, "Please rise for our national anthem." The game was about to start.

Six

It was now time for kickoff, and Bentley High had the ball first, so Violet was going to get to see her dad in action right away. The Cougars received the ball and made it all the way to the thirty-yard line. The team got into a huddle. Tommy had gotten the play from the coach and headed back from the sideline.

"Let's send these boys a message and get a score on the board right away. Flee flicker on one."

The team ran up to the ball, and Tommy chanted, "Down set...green eighty...green eighty...hit."

The center snapped the ball to Tommy, who handed it off to the running back, but there was some sort of trickery going on. The running back pitched the ball back to Tommy. Tommy looked down field, saw a man wide open, and let it go. Violet watched in awe as the ball went high into the air; it must've gone at least fifty yards. The wide receiver caught it in stride and ran it into the end zone.

"*Touchdown Cougars!*" yelled the announcer over the microphone. The Bentley High fans were going crazy.

The Falcons got the ball next, and they responded rather quickly. The score kept going back and forth. The Cougars would take the lead, and then the Falcons would take the lead.

This went on for the rest of the first half. Violet wanted her dad's team to win, but what mattered most to her was she was getting to experience her first football game, and in a way, it was with her dad.

I don't really know much about football, but I'd say my dad is really good, thought Violet.

The clock hit zero, and both teams exited the field because it was now halftime.

As her dad was exiting the field, he told the entire team to not say one word when they reached the locker room. *Is he going to give his team another speech?* thought Violet. Violet wanted to get closer and see what was going on, so she waited for the team to head into the locker room and snuck her way toward the target when the coast was clear. Violet knew she couldn't go in there, but the door was left open just enough for her to stick her head in and see what her dad had to say.

"Hey, great first half, offense, but I'm going to need the defense to step it up," explained Coach Detmer. "We're in a shootout right now. Their defense can't stop us. All we need to do is start making some big plays on defense, and the game is ours."

"Coach is right, but let me tell you something," said Tommy, "I know I didn't work this hard only to come this far and lose. I know you guys didn't either. What happens these next two quarters determines the season. What do we play this game for?"

"We play to win the game," the team responded in unison.

"That's right. We owe this win to this school, this town, and, most importantly, to ourselves. So let's go out there and get this *W*," Tommy concluded.

Halftime was over. The teams started to pour out of the locker room and onto the field. Violet made her way back to the sideline before anyone from the team was able to notice where she had been. Before kickoff, Tommy called his offense over.

"We can't control how the defense plays, but we can control how we play. Let's keep it going, and everything else will take care of itself."

Since the Cougars received the ball at the beginning of the game, the Falcons would get the ball now. The Cougars' defense didn't improve, though. They kept giving up yards, which led to touchdowns. Tommy knew that he was going to have to put the team on his back and lead them to victory. The Cougars' offense had an answer for every drive, and Tommy threw touchdown after touchdown.

The fourth quarter came, and the game was tied. The Falcons ended up taking their first lead of the night with two minutes left. It was now fifty-one to forty-four, and the Cougars had to make a quick drive if they wanted to tie this game and possibly go to overtime. The Cougars returned the ball to the thirty-five-yard line, which set them up for good field position. Tommy dropped back for his first pass of the drive and completed it for ten yards. The team didn't huddle, though, and Tommy was hurrying them up to the line. The next pass was for fifteen yards, and again Tommy ran up to the line and spiked the ball to stop the clock. There were fifty seconds left in the game, and the crowd was going wild. Violet couldn't contain her excitement either. She was in for quite the finish. Tommy got everyone lined up, ran the play, rolled right, and found a man open at the thirty. The wide receiver took the ball to the twenty, got knocked out of bounds, and the clock stopped with five seconds remaining.

After Tommy got the play from Coach Detmer, he lined everyone up. They had another trick play up their sleeves. Tommy snapped the ball and pitched it to the running back. He got in front, acting like he was going to lead block, and kept going down the field. At the very last moment, the running back stopped before he got past the line of scrimmage and threw the ball to the wide receiver on the other side of the field, who found Tommy wide open for a Cougar touchdown. The score was now fifty-one to fifty; all the Cougars needed was a field goal to tie up the game and send it to overtime. Coach Detmer sent the field goal unit out, but Tommy waved them off. He wanted to go for two and win the game.

This was it—a chance to keep their season alive and head to the state finals. Violet couldn't bear to watch and had her fingers crossed. Tommy lined the team up, this time in shotgun formation. The center snapped him the ball, and Tommy dropped it. The play was now broken, but Tommy picked the ball up and headed to the left corner of the end zone. It looked like a defensive player was going to be able to tackle Tommy before he made it into the end zone, but he reached for the pylon as he dove and won the game for the Bentley High Cougars.

"The two-point conversion is good! Cougars win! Cougars win!" yelled the announcer.

"He did it! He did it!" Violet exclaimed as she jumped up and down with joy.

The team rushed the field and started to pile onto Tommy. Shortly after, the fans stormed the field as well.

This is my chance, thought Violet, so she stormed the field too. Violet thought she was going to be able to speak with her father, but there were too many people in front of her. Again it wasn't a good time. She was going to have to find the right moment. Tommy arose from the pile of players and was bombarded by all the fans. They hugged him and gave him high fives; he was soon surrounded by newspaper reporters.

"Tommy, you just won the game and put your team into the state finals. What do you have to say?" one of them asked.

"Hey, I didn't do this on my own. I may have thrown all those touchdowns and ran in the game-winning two-point conversion, but I couldn't have done that without my line blocking for me and my receivers and running backs coming up with some big plays," Tommy responded.

"You think you'll bring home the title this year?" asked the same reporter.

"We're just taking this one game at a time. We practiced hard all week. It paid off, and we got the win. We're going to celebrate tonight, and come Monday, it's back to business," replied Tommy.

Wow, my dad's a hero, thought Violet as she turned around and headed off the field. Violet knew that she was more than likely not going to be able to have a chance to talk with her dad right now, so she headed for the gate. Violet was going to head to Lucy and Mark's house to check in with them, so she would be able to confirm that she had a place to stay. However, something told her that she should wait around for a bit. Violet saw a large group of fans and figured that they were hoping to interact with Tommy, so she waited beside them. A lot of them had pieces of paper and pens, intending to get his autograph, but Violet didn't have either. This was Violet's chance, and she needed a reason to go up to Tommy. So she had to improvise. Tommy was approaching; she had to act fast. Violet snatched a piece of paper from one fan, a pen from another, and quickly made her way to the front to ask Tommy for his autograph.

"Could you sign this for me?" asked Violet.

"You got it," replied Tommy. "Hey, I'm pretty sure I know you."

"Yeah, I'm in your environmental science class."

"That's right. Mr. Peterson was about to make you read in front of the class."

"Thanks for saving me from that. Really appreciate it."

"No problem. You were looking really uncomfortable, so I thought I would step in."

"Thanks for the autograph. I have to get home."

"What! Go home?"

Violet wanted to hang out with her dad more, but she just couldn't invite herself. She remembered that the waitress said that the football players always go celebrate their win at the diner, so she was hoping that her dad would extend an invite to her.

"I don't really know anybody, and plus the game really wore me out."

"You know me," said Tommy. "Hey, a bunch of us are going to go celebrate the win at the Old Town Diner, and you should come."

"That sounds like fun. All that cheering has given me an appetite, so I'm in."

"Cool. Just wait in the parking lot, and you can hitch a ride with me and my good buddy Brian."

Violet was heading to the parking lot as her dad kept signing autographs. She turned around to get another look at all the fans around him and couldn't help but be proud of her father. *My dad's a hero to all these people.* Her dad was indeed a hero, but the events that were going to take place later that night were going to show Violet that not only was he a hero on the field but also off the field.

About ten minutes later, Tommy arrived in the parking lot to meet Violet. They walked over to his truck, and standing right by it was Brian.

Could this be the Brian that he hung out with as a kid? Violet asked herself.

"Great game, and what a play to win it," said Brian as he congratulated Tommy.

"Thanks, bud! That means a lot," replied Tommy.

They all piled into Tommy's truck and were off to go celebrate at the diner. Brian asked Tommy about Violet, and Tommy explained that they shared a class. He added that she was new, and he wanted to show her a good time. They arrived at the diner and were greeted by more fans.

"The man, the myth, the legend!" exclaimed Brian as they were heading inside.

As soon as Tommy came in, everyone stood up and applauded. Even the owner of the restaurant came over to Tommy and told him that no matter what happened next week, he'd never have to pay for a meal here ever again.

I want free food. I could get a life supply of strawberry waffles, thought Violet.

Tommy was exceptionally modest in the face of all the praise and instead of gloating, he just humbly thanked everyone for their support and took a seat at an open booth.

"So, how long have you and Brian known each other?" asked Violet.

"We've been good friends since we were kids," replied Tommy.

"There were four others, but they all eventually moved away," added Brian.

"I'm sorry. That had to be hard. I could imagine it's not easy saying goodbye to friends," Violet responded.

"Yeah, but it makes you not take things for granted. You and your friends could be hanging out one day and not even know that it's your last," said Brian.

"That's true. I never thought about it that way. It's still sad that they're gone, though," acknowledged Violet.

"You know, my dad used to tell me that if you hold up five fingers and you can count at least one good friend, then you're doing all right. That's what I have in Brian," said Tommy.

"Really thankful for Tommy. He's a solid friend. We've been there for each other, both good times and bad times," added Brian.

Violet was inspired by Tommy and Brian's friendship. It made her think of Isabella.

I could have that too. Violet knew she had messed up by pushing Isabella away and snapping at her in the hallway. She wanted to fix things with Isabella but didn't know exactly how.

"Other than coming here, what else do you do for fun around this town?" asked Violet.

"There's the drive-in, a mall, an arcade, and Lake Lure Beach. Other than that, it's a small town with not much to do," replied Tommy.

"It's one of those towns where everybody knows everybody," added Brian.

"Could we go to the beach after this?" asked Violet.

"Yeah! We could toss around the football too," replied Tommy.

"Hey, you forgot one more thing that everyone does for fun around here—Sunset Peak," added Brian.

"What's that?" asked Violet.

"It's where people go to watch the sunset, but that's not all they do. It's about fifty feet above the water, and so some jump off it," explained Tommy.

"That's insane!" said Violet.

"Brian and I jumped on our sixteenth birthdays. It's kind of a tradition around here," said Tommy.

"It makes you feel reborn in a way. You jump from high up into the water and come out a new person," added Brian.

"Hey, let's get on out of here and make our way to the beach," Tommy indicated that he was ready to go.

He said his goodbyes and signed some more autographs on the way out. Then they were off to the beach.

I get to play catch with my dad, Violet thought as she stuck her head out the window to feel the breeze. Violet couldn't wait to get to the beach, but in the meantime, she would enjoy all the attention her father was getting. Every time they stopped at a light, cars would honk. People were wearing his jersey number, and some kids even got out of their parents' cars to run up to his truck and ask for an autograph. Violet was finding out more and more about her father and couldn't have been prouder of him.

Seven

A few minutes later, they arrived at the beach. Violet stood still at first, taking in the nighttime scenery. She was taken aback by how gorgeous the moonlit sky made the beach and lake look. The waves were calm now, and it added a soothing sound as they came to shore. Violet remembered how beautiful the beach was during the day on her first journey, but what she was experiencing now was incomparable. Everything looked so magical and gave Violet a carefree vibe. The night was young, and Violet felt as if she had all the time in the world to spend with her father.

Tommy reached for his football and told Brian to go long. Violet didn't really know how to play catch, so she just watched Tommy and Brian throw the football back and forth for a while; that was, until Tommy asked Violet if she wanted to join in.

"Thanks, but I don't know how to," Violet responded.

"Come over here, and I'll show you," said Tommy.

Violet's dad was really going to teach her how to play catch. This was something that she'd only been able to dream of, but now it was actually happening.

"Okay, hold the ball by the laces, put your arm back, point your elbow for accuracy, and let it go." Just like that, Tommy completed a perfect pass to Brian. "You ready to learn how to catch?" asked Tommy.

Violet smiled at Tommy and nodded yes.

"Open up your hands, put your two thumbs and pointer fingers together to make the shape of a diamond and look the ball in with your eyes as you're catching it," said Tommy. Brian threw the ball back to Tommy, and he made it all look so easy.

"Now it's your turn," said Tommy.

Violet gave it a shot. She did exactly what her dad had told her to do and made the perfect throw. Now it was time to catch it.

"Oh, and one more thing. Don't try to reach for the ball. You could end up jamming your fingers; so let it come to you."

Again, Violet did everything her dad had told her to do and was able to catch it.

"Hey, you got it!" said Tommy.

Tommy wanted to continue playing catch, but Brian said he was getting tired and ready to go home. Violet didn't want to leave. She wanted to play catch with her dad a little longer and asked if they could stay. Tommy was Brian's ride home, but Brian told them not to worry about it and said he could always just walk back to his house. Brian mentioned that they could meet back here tomorrow first thing in the morning, but Tommy said he had a doctor's appointment and could hang out later in the morning.

Violet and Tommy continued to throw the football back and forth well into the night. They talked and talked for hours. Tommy didn't really know Violet, so he asked her some questions.

"So tell me a little about yourself."

"I'm an only child, and my home life is pretty good."

"What about your mom and dad?"

"Mom loves me and is doing the best she can, but I've been giving her a hard time lately."

"And your dad?"

"I'm slowly realizing that he's my hero and someone I can look up to." That comment was directed at Tommy, but he had no idea he was having a conversation with his daughter. "I just wish he would come home though. I miss him."

"Does he go on vacations or business trips a lot?"

"You could say that," replied Violet

"Let's get going, though. I have a doctor's appointment early in the morning and we have a big day tomorrow, so we should get some sleep. I can take you home."

Tommy and Violet hopped in his truck. Violet gave Tommy directions to the house where she was staying. A couple of streets later, Violet noticed some smoke in the air and told Tommy that they should check it out. Tommy turned into a subdivision and followed the smoke. When they pulled up, they saw that a house was on fire.

"There are people in that house," said Violet with a trembling tone in her voice.

"We have to get out and help," Tommy echoed her feelings.

Tommy and Violet got out of the car and started running toward the house. They had to go in and save those people before it was too late. There were people standing in the street outside the house yelling for help but not doing anything. Tommy yelled for everyone to step aside and, without any thought, ran inside the house. Violet could only look on in a panic as she waited for her dad to emerge from the fire. He then came out with what appeared to be a middle-aged lady and man. The lady and man pleaded with Tommy to head back inside the house because their daughter was still in there. Tommy told Violet to take the woman and man to safety and ran back into the house. Once again Violet had to worry about her father, but before she knew it Tommy came out with a girl who looked to be about their age in his arms.

The house was ruined, but lives were saved. The mom, dad and their daughter couldn't thank them enough.

My dad didn't even know those people and risked his life for them, thought Violet. Tommy approached Violet, and she expressed to him that it was one of the bravest things she'd ever seen anyone do.

"I'm glad you're okay," said Violet as she gave her dad a big hug.

"Let's get you home now," said Tommy.

Tommy and Violet were now on their way to Lucy and Mark's house. Violet was excited to see them once again. Their note had read, "See you soon!" Maybe they were expecting her. That could also mean that she'd be more than welcome to come back anytime she wanted. Yet something didn't add up, and Violet was in for a big surprise. They pulled up to the house, and Tommy reminded Violet to meet them at the beach tomorrow morning. They both said their goodbyes, and Violet made her way to the door.

"I'm back," Violet shouted as she opened the front door, but there was no reply. *Maybe they're out celebrating, too, and haven't made their way back yet.* Violet took a seat on the couch and made herself at home. Something didn't seem right to her as she looked around. She noticed that the walls had been repainted, and it looked like furniture had been moved around. The place didn't look the same as she remembered. *They must've done some touching up. My mom does it all the time.* Violet saw some pictures over by a shelf and headed over to check them out. *I've never seen these before.* She noticed these pictures were of a family she didn't recognize, and it hit her that Lucy and Mark didn't live there anymore.

Suddenly a light went on upstairs. "Who's down there?" a man called out.

Violet started to panic, made her way out the sliding door into the back yard, and hopped the fence.

What is going on? Why would they say "see you soon" if they knew they weren't going to be there? None of this made sense to Violet. Now she didn't have a place to stay, and she was all alone. She knew that her dad would more than likely give her a place to stay, but she had forgotten where he lived. Violet was going to have to figure out where she was going to sleep, so she wandered off into the night.

I'll just go sleep on the beach. She was supposed to meet Tommy and Brian there in the morning anyway, so why not? Before she got to the beach, a stray dog approached her. It was a brown and black German Shepherd, and it looked like it had been trying to find its way home too.

"Hey, boy, you don't have a home either?" said Violet.

The dog stood there wagging its tail and was really excited to see Violet. It even jumped up and tried to lick Violet on the face.

"I don't have one either, so it's okay."

The dog let out a bark, spun in a circle twice, and then jumped into Violet's arms.

"You want to keep me company on the beach, I see," said Violet. The dog let out two barks. Violet took that as a yes. Looks like Violet wasn't going to be on her own after all.

Sleeping on the beach didn't seem that bad to Violet. The moon and stars were out, and the weather was pretty warm. Violet and the stray got to the beach. Violet had to find them a good place to sleep. She saw a beach blanket that someone had left behind, so they set up there. As soon as Violet lay down, the dog came and cuddled right next to her. Violet felt protected by the stray dog. It reminded her of Buster's habit of providing comfort by sleeping next to her when it was storming. Violet was once again mesmerized by the full moon and all of the stars. She wanted to fall asleep, but everything just looked so enchanting to her. Violet started playing connect the dots with the stars and saw that she could make some interesting figures. She noticed that one figure mimicked the shape of an item her mom used in the kitchen but couldn't come up with the name of it.

"We'll find your home first thing in the morning. My dad is the nicest person, and I know he'll help. Just wait till you meet him," Violet said to the dog. She began trying to count all the stars in the sky and fell asleep in the process.

Violet was awoken by the bright sun. She opened her eyes, and the first thing she noticed was that the stray dog was gone. She sat up and looked around, but the dog was nowhere to be found. She started whistling, calling out to the dog; still nothing.

Hope he's able to find his way home. Let's see if Tommy and Brian are here yet. Violet went to the parking lot of the beach and only saw Brian, not Tommy.

"Where's Tommy?" asked Violet.

"Remember? He said he had a doctor's appointment and would be running late," replied Brian.

"That's right."

Violet could tell that Brian wasn't too good at small talk, so she brought up what happened last night to make the conversation more interesting.

"The craziest thing happened last night."

"If you're going to tell me about how Tommy saved that family from the fire last night, then I already know," Brian said. "It was on the news, and I read all about it in the paper this morning"

"Really heroic of him."

"Yeah, but I'm not surprised. Tommy's the most selfless person I know."

Tommy had pulled up in his truck, and Violet noticed that he didn't look like his chipper self.

"Come on, you guys. Let's go," said Tommy in a grumpy manner.

Violet became really concerned. Her dad had just won the game for his team last night and then he saved an entire family from a burning house. *If I had accomplished all those things, I would feel like I was on top of the world*, she thought.

"Where are we going?" asked Brian.

"Let's just go get some breakfast, and we'll go from there."

On the way to breakfast, Tommy didn't say much and even Brian seemed concerned.

"You okay, Tommy? You haven't really said a word."

"I'll explain everything at breakfast," said Tommy.

They didn't go to the Old Town Diner this time. They decided to go to a drive-in breakfast place called Dan's Grab 'N Go. Tommy didn't want to be around many people, so he thought it would be best to hang out in the car for a while.

When they got there, they ordered right away, but Tommy wasn't too hungry; he only got coffee. Right when they parked, Tommy couldn't hold it in much longer and delivered the news.

"After the state title game, my football playing days are over." His voice was filled with disappointment.

Brian and Violet could only stare at Tommy in shock and didn't really know what to say. Tommy had played the game of a lifetime last night, and now he apparently wouldn't be playing ever again.

"Why? What happened?" asked Brian in disbelief.

"I rather not talk about it now. I'm not ready to."

"Was it something the doctor told you?" asked Violet.

"I made a promise to my dad and played my heart out for him every game, and now it's over. I don't even know how I'm going to tell him. I'm at a loss right now," Tommy's head hung low.

"Don't worry, Tommy. We'll get through this together, just like we've gotten through everything else. I'm here for you," said Brian.

Tommy broke down and clung onto Violet and Brian. Tommy was in pain, and who could blame him? Seeing that Brian was Tommy's best friend, he knew exactly what would get his mind off of things for the moment.

"I know what will cheer you up."

"What's that?" asked Tommy.

"Let's go jump off of Sunset Peak," Brian said excitedly.

"Yeah, let's all do it," said Tommy.

Violet took a deep gulp because she was scared of heights. She had swung with her dad on the rope into the lake at the secret hangout spot, but this was completely different. Fifty feet up was a long way down.

"I'll just watch."

"Nonsense! We're all going," said Brian.

"Come on, Violet. It will be fun," Tommy added.

"It's perfectly safe. We've been doing it since we were sixteen," Brian attempted to reassure her.

On the way to Sunset Peak, Violet was contemplating whether or not she wanted to jump. *What if I do this and get hurt?* thought Violet, but then she remembered that her dad had ran into the burning house despite the high risk of injury or even death. Violet again thought about how high the peak was, and by the time they arrived at the chosen spot, she couldn't convince herself to jump.

"There it is, and not many people are up there, so there won't be a long wait," said Brian.

"You coming, Violet?" asked Tommy.

Violet looked up all the way to the top of the peak and took an even bigger gulp. "I'll be right behind you."

"I'm going to run up there. I'll see you guys at the top," said Brian.

Violet and Tommy wanted to take their time, and this gave Violet another chance to speak with her father.

"I'm really sorry that you can't play football anymore."

"It's fine. I got so caught up in my emotions that I forgot about one thing."

"What's that?"

"God has a plan for everything."

"What do you mean by that?"

"God could have something greater for me out there. I just have to have faith."

"Have you ever seen God?"

"No, I haven't."

"Why believe in something that you can't see?"

Violet thought she was being clever with her questions. But Tommy knew exactly what to say, even though his words would fall on deaf ears again.

"Believing isn't seeing. It's by faith."

There was that phrase again that she had heard from her mom. "How can someone expect me to have faith in something that's not real?" Violet then thought of a smart remark, but it turned out to not be effective as she had expected. "Well, I've never seen Santa Claus and growing up, I had faith that he was real. Look how that turned out. At least I was given presents. What had this so-called God ever given me?" Violet used a condescending tone.

All Tommy could do was smirk. He realized he wasn't getting anywhere with this.

"Look, Violet, I can't convince you of this. It's something that you'll have to figure out for yourself. My hope is that our conversation has spiked some curiosity in you and you start to ask questions."

"Whatever you say," said Violet sarcastically.

"Hey, we're here to have fun, though. We can always save this conversation for another time. That's if you'd like to."

Tommy and Violet reached the top, but there were a couple people in front of them, so they had to wait for a while.

Violet looked ahead in fear; as the line got shorter, she started shaking. As soon as they reached the front and it was their turn to go, Violet started freaking out. "I don't think I can do this," she said in a panic.

"You're scared of heights, aren't you?"

"Yeah...I am." Violet was ashamed.

"It's okay to be scared. You just have to be brave."

"That's easy for you to say. You never seem scared."

Tommy could only laugh to himself again. "Violet, my heart was pounding so hard when I ran into that house to save that family. Honestly, I've never seen myself as being able to do something like that, but you have to be brave. You can't stand in the background all the time. You have to live life and take chances."

This made Violet's ears perk up, and she saw that this bit of advice was relevant to more than just jumping off the peak. She saw this as a way of being able to move forward with her friendship with Isabella and stop being so cautious when it came to putting herself out there. The idea that this message could have a much deeper meaning never crossed her mind. Violet had chosen her path, and she was willing to see it through to the end.

Violet still had her doubts about herself. Once again, she made herself vulnerable and reached out to her dad for help.

"I don't think I can. I don't know how to."

"All people are braver than they think. They just have to take a leap of faith and find the bravery." Tommy smiled at Violet. "See you at the bottom."

Tommy went off the edge of the peak and dove into the water.

It was now Violet's turn. Right when she looked over the edge, she backed up in terror.

Come on, Violet, you can do this. If you don't start now, when will you? Violet said to herself. It was now or never, and Violet had to choose quickly because others who were waiting started to grow impatient.

"All right, I'll go on three," said Violet. "One...two... three."

She took a deep breath and jumped. It may have seemed like forever to Violet, but it didn't take long for her to reach the bottom; she went deep into the water. Right away she tried to swim back up but couldn't. The more she tried to swim to the surface, the more she felt pulled under and kept sinking.

Eight

It was now Thursday morning and time for Isabella to wake up and get ready for school. She got up earlier than most kids because she had a daily morning routine: get in the shower, have her mom brush her hair, read scripture and pray with her family, and last, have a family breakfast. Isabella was brought up in a loving Christian household. Both of her parents made it their jobs to make sure that Isabella knew God growing up; they made sure she had the best of everything and always encouraged her to be the best she could. They were there for her through the good times and the bad. Her parents always provided shoulders that she could lean on and cry on.

When Isabella was seven years old, she was diagnosed with cancer. Going to church every Sunday morning and hearing her dad preach played an influential part in her life during this time. It made her faith stronger, and it helped her get through a dark period. She lost hope at times but would turn to God to restore that hope. One Sunday at church, the whole congregation prayed over her for hours. Not even a week later, she was cancer-free.

At the breakfast table with her family, Isabella reflected on those times, and this helped her make sense of what might be going on with Violet. The other day, Violet had dismissed her comment about God right away and had become angry with Isabella in the hallway when in fact she was only trying to comfort Violet.

Violet must be going through something and has completely lost hope, thought Isabella. Isabella wanted to help Violet out and give back after all the help she had received. The only problem was that Violet kept avoiding her and made it clear that she wanted Isabella to stay away. Isabella knew only one person who could solve this—her father.

"I need help with something," she said to her dad.

"What's wrong?" asked Pastor Evans.

"There's this girl named Violet at school, and I think she's going through a rough patch in her life. I want to be there for her, but she pushes me away."

"Maybe she's ashamed and doesn't want to talk about it."

"But why push me away? I was only trying to be her friend."

"The closer you get to her, the more you could potentially find out."

"I've never thought about it that way. It must be something big," replied Isabella. "I also made a comment about God, and she lashed out at me later on that day."

"Whatever she's going through, she must be angry at God about it. Just leave her be for now."

"You mean don't be her friend?"

"No. Let me tell you a story, so it makes more sense."

Pastor Evans told Isabella the story about the prodigal son. It was about a father who had two sons. One of them asked for the portion of the goods he felt entitled to and then took off. As the son was on his journey, he ran out of what his father had given him and saw that what he had done was wrong. The father waited patiently for his son to return and saw him approaching in the distance. Now the father could've been mad at his son, but instead he ran up to him, gave him a hug, put his best robe around him, and told his servant to slaughter their best calf so they could celebrate the son's return. Pastor Evans continued to explain to Isabella that even though the father was hurt by the son's actions, he still welcomed him back with open arms. He waited patiently. Isabella might have been confused and hurt by Violet's actions, but the moral of this story was to be loving, understanding, and welcoming when the time was right.

"Thanks, Dad. That makes a lot more sense."

"Hey, that's what I'm here for," replied Pastor Evans. "Also, you may have planted a seed by even bringing up God, and we don't know if whether others have planted some too. You have to remember that it's all in God's timing when those seeds will start to grow."

Isabella's concerns had been answered, but she still couldn't help but worry about Violet. She had been taught to love all and wanted to love Violet.

Guess she's just not ready yet, thought Isabella as they continued on with the family breakfast until it was time to head to school.

—⧓—

Violet plopped right into her bed and then rolled off onto the floor, which caused a loud thump. She got up and looked around; Violet knew she was back in her room but wanted to make sure. She ran over to her mirror to get a good look at herself: Violet looked like Violet again.

Phew, I'm back again, and I'm me this time. She was relieved. Her mother was knocking on the door.

"I heard a loud crash and then some running. Everything okay in there?"

"Yeah, just a crazy dream. I'll tell you about it later."

The falling out of bed made sense, but the running didn't. *What is my daughter up to?* Mrs. Cooper asked herself. She thought about it and concluded, *Kids will be kids.* She started heading downstairs.

Meanwhile, Violet felt as if she had been gone for a long period. Before her mother had made it all the way down the stairs, she opened the door to ask what day it was.

"It's Thursday," her mom said with a confused look on her face.

"That's right."

"That must've been some dream and fall. You sure you're okay?" Mrs. Cooper was again concerned.

"Yeah, Mom, I'm just getting my days mixed up. That's all. I'll see you downstairs." *Hmm. . .maybe these sessions with Mrs. Turner have been a lot,* thought Violet's mom.

Violet was in a hurry because she wanted to get to school right away. She had felt like she developed a new perspective on life and had a feeling that today was going to be a lot different. She raced to get her clothes on, got all her belongings in her backpack, and was ready to move on with the day. Her mom had breakfast ready on the table, but Violet insisted that she should take it to go, so she could get to school right away. *What has gotten into her?* Violet's mom asked herself as she wrapped up the egg and bacon sandwich in a napkin and then headed out the door.

On the way to school, Violet's mom asked her about her dream.

"So what was that dream you had?"

Violet was afraid that she was going to spill her secret, but her mom thought it was only a dream. "Dad ran into this house that was on fire and saved a mom, dad and their daughter."

Mrs. Cooper was struck with surprise. She knew the scenario well; *she* was the daughter that Violet's dad had carried out.

"Violet, I was the daughter that your dad carried to safety."

"That's how you and Dad met?"

"Yeah, and I fell in love with him right away."

"That's so neat. Maybe you could tell me more about that tonight."

Jennifer saw this as another opportunity for her and her daughter to try to bond even more. She was surprised that Violet actually wanted to hear more about her father. Just the other day, she didn't even want to step foot in the park where she, Violet, and Violet's dad had created some memorable moments. Now she wanted to hear the full story of how her mom and dad fell in love.

"I would love to share more about your father and me. You sure about this, though? I know how you felt about our visit to the park yesterday, so I just want to make sure."

"That was really cool how he saved you from that fire. Sure...why not."

Violet always had been a fan of love stories. When she was a little girl, she and her mother used to watch Disney movies such as *The Little Mermaid, Cinderella, Aladdin, Tangled, Sleeping Beauty* and *Snow White* where the princess is in distress, ends up getting saved by the prince they've been waiting for, and they fall in love. To Violet, her mom was the princess that was in trouble and her dad was the prince that saved the day. This connection is what sparked Violet's interest in the first place.

"Looking forward to spending time with you tonight and hearing yours and dads love story."

"Looking forward to some mother-daughter time too. Love you to the moon and back."

"I love you to the moon and back too, Mom."

She's saying "I love you more," we're spending more time together, and she actually wants to hear more about her father. God, I still don't know what you're doing, but thank you, thought Violet's mom as she watched her beloved daughter head into school. She could be getting her daughter back after all.

Violet was rushing into the building and was going so fast that she didn't even bother to say hello to Isabella as they crossed paths. Isabella looked back at Violet to see if she had even noticed her, but Violet kept on going. Isabella had to accept what her dad had told her and be patient.

Violet arrived at her classroom, and as usual, Mrs. Summers was there to greet her.

"Hello, Violet. I'm really glad to see you," Her voice was pleasant.

"Can't talk now; I want to be ready for Mrs. Turner."

Well, that's a first, thought Mrs. Summers. Violet had always dreaded seeing Mrs. Turner, but something in her was changing. This transformation in Violet was happening so fast that Mrs. Summers didn't know what to expect, but she suspected that it was going to be positive.

"Violet, I really like your attitude this morning."

"What do you mean?" asked Violet with a confused look on her face.

"You always seem so down when you come in, but today you have a lot of energy and look like you're ready to take on the world."

"Yeah, I guess you're right."

"Hey, Violet, could you give Mrs. Turner this note?"

Violet did feel like she was ready to take on anything, though what was inside the note would make her think otherwise.

"Will do," replied Violet as she went skipping down the hallway to go see Mrs. Turner.

As usual, Mrs. Turner's door was closed, so Violet knocked, and shortly after, Mrs. Turner let her in. Violet went up to her and handed her the folded-up piece of paper, then went to go sit in her usual spot. Mrs. Turner opened the note: "Read a Dr. Seuss book to class and Violet had a nervous breakdown."

"Can we start? I would love to tell you about my story so far," said Violet. That was the real reason she wanted to rush to Mrs. Turner—to tell her more about her story.

Mrs. Turner had other plans for Violet. "I'm glad that you're still writing, but let's switch things up a bit today."

"We'll talk about it at the end, I guess," replied Violet.

What Mrs. Turner was about to ask Violet was going to weigh heavily on her heart, and it was going to take a lot of strength to address this. Mrs. Turner was prepared for Violet to start acting out but was hoping for the best.

"Mrs. Summers told me that you had a panic attack while she was reading Dr. Seuss to the class. Could you tell me a little more about that?"

Violet was looking around and was trying to come up with an excuse. "It was just hot in the classroom, and I needed some fresh air," she responded in a nervous tone.

"Violet, we both know that's not true. That Dr. Seuss book means something to you, doesn't it? Possibly about your father?"

Violet started to shake her leg uncontrollably, a sign that things were getting uncomfortable for her.

"It's okay to be scared. You just have to be strong," Mrs. Turner continued.

Violet started to get an eye full of tears and slowly let it out. "My...my...dad."

"Go on Violet. You're doing good. It's okay."

"He...he read it to me every night till I fell asleep. It was our thing," said Violet as she cried. "I remember when I was little, I would sit at the bottom of the stairs at night with my Dr. Seuss book waiting for him to come home and read it to me..."

Mrs. Turner went over to Violet and started rubbing her back in an effort to comfort her. "It makes me miss him so much...reminds me that he's gone, and I didn't even get to say goodbye," continued Violet. Right when Violet said this last part, she could no longer speak and wept hysterically in Mrs. Turner's arms.

Mrs. Turner regretted having to poke at sensitive issues that would tug on Violet's heart, but she knew it was the only way to help. Suppressing a memory and not dealing with the emotions that came with it was a recipe for disaster. Mrs. Turner knew exactly what to do to help Violet deal with this.

"Violet, look at me," said Mrs. Turner. Violet wiped the tears from her eyes but still had a look of despair on her face. "What emotions did you feel when your father read you Dr. Seuss?"

"Pure happiness, joy, and excitement."

Mrs. Turner wanted to teach Violet how to turn a negative into a positive. Violet once had a positive experience with the Dr. Seuss book, but now she correlated it with her father being gone. Mrs. Turner could also tell that Violet had a negative outlook on life, her sense of self included, and she needed to get Violet to break the cycle.

"Violet, every time you see a Dr. Seuss book, I want you to think about the positive experience you had, the joy that it brought you," said Mrs. Turner. "This goes for everything else: don't think about the negatives, and find the beauty in everything."

"I should try to think happy thoughts and not think the worst of everything?"

"There are going to be times in life where you do have bad thoughts, but you can't let it control or define you."

Mrs. Turner could see in Violet's eyes that she'd had enough and ended the session early. This was another big milestone for Violet because she'd opened up in a big way. Mrs. Turner was trying to get Violet to feel more comfortable talking about her father, so she could address what she was feeling and accept the truth that she'd been avoiding for quite some time. What happened in today's session was a big step in the right direction, so she was really looking forward to their next session.

"You did really well today, Violet. I'm extremely proud of you," she said. "Sorry we didn't get to your story."

"It's okay. I'm not finished anyway."

"Enjoy the rest of your day and think positive. If you need anything else, you know where to find me."

Violet left, and Mrs. Turner went over to her desk to jot down some things from today's session. On the way over, she kept thinking, *She's finally starting to open up about her father. Is this you, God?* Mrs. Turner felt someone hugging her from behind, and when she turned her head to see who it was, she saw it was Violet.

"Thanks, Mrs. Turner, and sorry for ruining your picture," said Violet graciously before quickly leaving.

This is God, thought Mrs. Turner.

Violet got back to the classroom. The students were paired up for a reading workshop, but Violet didn't feel like reading. She was still emotionally exhausted from her session with Mrs. Turner and needed some time to wind down. Mrs. Summers saw Violet walk in and went toward her. She could tell by the look in Violet's eyes that it had been a rough session and she needed support.

"Violet, glad to have you back. Would you like to find a partner to read with? You can read with me if you'd like."

"I'm not really in the mood right now. Could I work on my story?"

"Yeah, that's fine. You want to bring your stuff up here and work at my desk by me?"

"I would like that a lot."

Violet went back to her seat to get her stuff. Mrs. Summers had become overwhelmed with excitement. *Violet has barely said a word to me all year—until now,* thought Mrs. Summers. This was her chance to attempt to connect with Violet.

Violet sat down across from Mrs. Summers and started to get to work. Periodically Mrs. Summers caught Violet smiling at her, and she pleasantly smiled back. She was still curious as to what Violet was working on. Because Mrs. Summers wrote children's books, this topic was her way of finding common ground with Violet.

"How's your story coming?"

"The parts of the story about the adventures that the girl goes on are really good, but I have a feeling that the ending is going to be even better."

"You know, I write stories in my spare time and would love to hear the whole thing."

"You write stories, like an author?"

"I've had several children's books published over the years."

"That's so cool. You're, like, famous or something. Like a movie star. You must get driven in a limo to school every day."

Mrs. Summers didn't know what to say to that, but it did make her laugh. *She's so adorable and funny, and she doesn't even know it.*

As a part of the writers' workshop in the afternoon, students were going to be given an opportunity to share their work with the class. Mrs. Summers wanted Violet to participate more, and here was her chance.

"Violet, would you like to share your project with the class during the writing workshop?" asked Mrs. Summers.

Violet sat there for a while contemplating the question, and Mrs. Summers kept trying to encourage her.

"Come on, Violet. I bet you're a good writer."

"I'll think about it but can't promise you anything," replied Violet before going back to her writing.

That answer's better than the usual, thought Mrs. Summers.

Nine

The bell sounded, and it was time for all the kids to head to lunch. Violet wanted to find Isabella in order to make things right. When she got to the cafeteria, she looked around for Isabella. She spotted her, but she was sitting with other kids.

She's found new friends. I'm too late! Violet thought frantically. Violet wanted to join them, but there was no room, so she went to go sit at a table alone. Throughout the lunch period, Violet kept looking at Isabella and all her new friends. This made her feel deep regret about her treatment of Isabella. A friendship that once seemed promising now seemed like it was gone.

Why do I always end up ruining everything? Violet angrily thought to herself.

It was now time for recess, but Violet had other plans. She was going to take Mrs. Turner up on her offer and go see her again. Even though Violet thought she'd completely ruined her friendship with Isabella, she wondered whether there was something she could do to fix it. Mrs. Turner had helped her out this far, so perhaps she could in this instance too. If anyone had an answer for a problem like this, it was Mrs. Turner. From Violet's perspective, she was an angel in disguise and always knew what to say. Mrs. Turner was surprised to see Violet since it was recess, but she was happy that Violet had come to her more for help.

"Not going outside today?"

"Didn't really feel like it."

"Won't your new friend miss you out there?"

"That's actually what I'm here for."

"Why don't you take a seat, and we can figure this out?"

"Think I ruined my friendship with Isabella," Violet started to sound ashamed.

"What happened?" Mrs. Turner asked with concern.

"Things were going good, and then she brought up God. I'm angry at him and don't exactly believe. I don't want her to find out that I don't have a dad. She would ask me questions, and then I'd have to talk about something that I'm just not ready to. I've been avoiding her because of it," Violet explained. "What if she doesn't want to be my friend when she finds out these things?"

"There you go again. You're thinking the worst of things," replied Mrs. Turner, "You don't know how she will respond. You're assuming this."

"That's what my mom told me."

"Your mom's right, and you won't know until you open up to Isabella. But instead you keep avoiding her because you think something negative is going to happen."

"I even got mad at her the other day when she was only trying to help me. She asked what was wrong, and I didn't want to tell her the real reason. It also looks like she's made some new friends."

"The friendship can't be over just like that. She's more than likely hurt, too, and wondering why you've been avoiding her. The thing is, she's done everything to extend her friendship to you, and now the ball's in your court."

"What does 'the ball's in your court' mean?"

"It means what happens next is up to you."

"How do I fix this?"

"Be honest with her. Spill everything. Apologize for what happened in the hallway. I've heard good things about Isabella, and she sounds like an understanding person."

"Thanks, Mrs. Turner," said Violet as she gave her another big hug. By the time they were done talking, recess was over so Violet had to head back to class. She was very much hoping that this was going to work. She needed and wanted Isabella back as a friend, but for now she was going to have to be patient and wait until school ended. When she got back to class, it was time for writers' workshop, and Violet was still thinking about whether she wanted to share her story or not.

"Okay, class, you've been working on your stories thus far, but now is the time you get to share with the class. Who would like to volunteer?" asked Mrs. Summers.

A couple of kids raised their hands, but not Violet. Mrs. Summers waited a little longer, but still Violet didn't raise her hand. Two students shared their stories, and meanwhile Mrs. Summers kept looking at Violet to see whether she was going to change her mind. But she didn't.

The last student shared, and Mrs. Summers asked the class, "Is there anyone else who would like to go? We still have a couple of minutes left before we move onto science." She looked at Violet. "Okay, going once, going twice, and..."

Before Mrs. Summers could tell the class that it was time to move on, Violet's hand shot up. All the students were shocked because typically Violet didn't even join them on the rug, let alone participate. Violet took a deep breath and headed to the front of the class. She was looking at the ground because she was nervous; she then started tapping her feet together. Mrs. Summers went up to her and whispered in her ear, "I believe in you." This calmed Violet's nerves, so she started sharing.

Violet explained to the class that her story was about a girl who really missed her father. She longed for the times that her and her father once had together. One day, though, she found a shoebox full of stuff her dad had left behind. These items were magical and made it possible for her to go on adventures with her dad. The kids seemed really fascinated by the story, and all were saying how cool that was. Not Mrs. Summers, though. She knew that the little girl in the story was Violet, and that her pupil was expressing how much she missed her dad. Mrs. Summers had to turn away for a bit to pull herself together and avoid crying in front of her students.

It must've taken a lot for Violet to share. It's good that she's expressing herself and not holding it in, thought Mrs. Summers.

When Violet was done, the kids all clapped for her and told her how good of a job she had done on the story. This helped Violet continue to come out of her shell. Things went smoothly the rest of the day.

The time to dismiss students came, and Violet was in a hurry because she wanted to talk with Isabella before they both headed home. On the way out, Mrs. Summers stopped Violet because she had something important to say.

"Violet, I'm really proud of your efforts today. You're really starting to blossom."

What Violet said back really tugged at Mrs. Summers's heartstrings.

"Thanks for caring even when you didn't have to," replied Violet, and off she went to go fix things with Isabella.

Now that the classroom was empty, Mrs. Summers could cry. They weren't tears of sadness; they were tears of joy. Violet was becoming the student Mrs. Summers always believed she could be.

When Violet got outside, she saw that Isabella was about to get on the bus, so she yelled, "Isabella, wait!" and rushed over to her. It took a while for Violet to get everything out, and she was just staring at Isabella. This was going to be hard, but she knew that it was necessary. "Isabella, I'm sorry I've been avoiding you and for lashing out at you in the hallway. I don't know what's going on with me, I'm scared…my dad…I don't know how I feel about God and…" Violet became hysterical. Before she could get anything else out, Isabella stopped her in her tracks. What she said gave Violet affirmation that Mrs. Turner and her mom had been right all along.

"Violet, I don't care about that. I just want to be your friend."

Violet was so relieved that she jumped for joy and gave Isabella a giant hug.

"So does that mean you'll come over today?" asked Isabella.

"I would love to," replied Violet. "My mom's waiting to pick me up. I have to go home first and eat, then I can come over later."

"Hey, you can have dinner with my family and me. You can also take the bus home with me too."

"That's a great idea. Wait here while I go ask my mom."

Violet spotted her mom's car and ran over to ask if she could go over to Isabella's, explaining that she would call later when she was ready to be picked up. Mrs. Cooper wasn't sure at first of how to respond. They were supposed to hang out that night and have their mother-daughter time, but Violet kept trying to persuade her mom.

"Please, please, please…We can always spend time together when I come home."

Mrs. Cooper couldn't say no. She was too caught up in the fact that Violet actually had a playdate with a friend. Day after day, Violet would come home and go to her room until dinner and, after that, head upstairs to bed, so this was a breath of fresh air for her.

"You can go, but have one of Isabella's parents give me a call as soon as you get there."

"Thanks, Mom, and will do. Love you."

Violet ran back to Isabella with excitement to tell her the good news and got on the bus to head to the Evans household. Isabella and Violet headed to the back of the bus. Sometimes, when Isabella would sit back here, she would turn around and make funny faces out the window at all the people in the cars behind them, so she wanted to get Violet in on the fun.

"You sure we won't get in trouble?" Violet asked nervously.

"Never once have I gotten in trouble. The worst that's happened was they made funny faces back," replied Isabella.

Isabella and Violet made faces for most of the ride home, and by the end they were in tears from laughing so hard.

"So what are your parents like?" asked Violet.

"Don't worry, Violet. They're the nicest, most down-to-earth people you'll meet," replied Isabella.

Isabella's stop had come, and Violet couldn't help but notice the man and woman who were standing there waving and holding welcome home signs with Isabella's name on them.

"Are those your parents?"

"That's them, all right."

"What's up with the signs?"

"They have a theme each day for when the bus drops me off at home."

"Never heard of this before."

"I'll have my parents tell you about their theme on the first day of school."

Isabella and Violet got off the bus and headed over to her parents. When Isabella's parents introduced themselves to Violet, she tried to shake their hands, but both parents insisted on giving her hugs because they always tried to give a warm welcome to a new acquaintance. As you might have imagined, Violet was pretty nervous about her first playdate, but the warm welcome calmed her nerves.

As they were walking the girls toward the front door, both parents asked how their days went. Violet and Isabella agreed that it was the best day ever, referring to what had happened at school that day. Violet had her best day yet at school this year. She was opening up more about her father and reaching out for help. Isabella was happy that she and Violet had resolved their issues and that a beautiful friendship had begun. Violet was curious herself about the theme Isabella's parents put together each day, so she began to inquire.

"Isabella told me you guys do something special for her every day when she gets home from school. Could you tell me more about that?"

"We saw a video on YouTube where these parents would have a different theme for the day for when their kid got home. They would dress up in different costumes and try to embarrass them as much as possible," said Pastor Evans.

"Isabella didn't like it at first but has gotten used to it," added Mrs. Evans.

"The first day of school was the most embarrassing of them all. My parents were waiting for me to get home in onesies. My mom was a panda, and my dad was a dinosaur," said Isabella as she put her palm to her face.

"That's hilarious" added Violet, before saying to herself, *This family is neat. I really like them.*

Once the group was settled in the house, Mr. and Mrs. Evans told the girls to have fun but to try to get some school work done first. Isabella explained to her parents that they both had a love for math and that this was actually a homework hangout. Isabella's parents added that they would call them for dinner in about an hour. As the girls headed upstairs to get started, Violet remembered that her mom wanted to speak with Pastor Evans.

"Pastor Evans, my mom wanted you to call her as soon as we got to your house. Here's the number."

"I would be more than happy to speak with her. You two run along now and don't have too much fun."

Isabella and Violet went upstairs to Isabella's room. They had just started long multiplication in class and wanted to quiz each other on what they had learned thus far. They both wrote out problems for the other to solve; they wanted to see who could finish first and with the higher degree of accuracy. Since this was still all new, they used the notes they had taken in class. Isabella had a lot of neat math manipulatives that helped them out. She was usually really good at math, but for once she was stumped, so Violet helped her out.

"Where do we start after the ones column?" asked Isabella.

"After you finish in the ones column, you place a zero there, and then you move into the tens column," replied Violet

"Oh, so when I'm done multiplying the number in the tens column, I place a zero there, so I don't get confused when I move onto the hundreds column?"

"That's right."

As Violet and Isabella continued working on math, Pastors Evans and Mrs. Cooper had a conversation of their own over the phone.

"Jennifer Cooper speaking. How can I help you?"

"Hello, Jennifer, this is Pastor Luke Evans. Your daughter Violet said you wanted to speak with me."

"Ah, yes, I just wanted to make sure they made it there safely. How's she doing, by the way?"

"She and Isabella are upstairs working on math and are going to have dinner soon. It sounds like they're having a good time up there," replied Pastor Luke reassuringly.

"I'm glad to hear it. It's been a rough time for Violet. Everything with her dad…she's had trouble making friends and has had a rough time at school and at home. I've tried talking to her about God, but she's really angry and has stopped believing," explained Mrs. Cooper. "I'm extremely thankful for your daughter reaching out to Violet. Also, for you showing her such great hospitality."

"We're really thankful for Violet too. She's welcome here anytime."

"Thank you so much. I don't know what to say."

"It's our pleasure. Also, I don't know the full extent with what's going on with Violet, but I will be praying for her. May God touch her and heal her."

"That means a lot. Thanks again. Could you also let Violet know that I'll be by to get her around eight and ask her to be ready?"

"Will do, and you have a good night."

Pastor Luke thought about the conversation he had with Mrs. Cooper. *How could such a sweet little girl be so angry at someone who's so loving?* Pastor Luke thought. Deep down inside he wanted to talk to Violet about God, but he was going to have to take baby steps. That included continuing to show her the love of God and continuing to be welcoming. Even including her in the prayer at dinner could plant another seed that could potentially grow. Pastor Luke was going to have to tread lightly because Violet was still in a fragile stage in her healing.

Mrs. Evans then told Luke that dinner was ready and asked him to call the girls down to wash their hands and head to the table. He called up to them and told them he and Mrs. Evans would be waiting at the table.

When Isabella and Violet took a seat at the table, everything looked ready to go, so Violet went to help herself but was stopped by Pastor Luke. He explained to Violet that before every meal in the Evans household that they prayed and gave thanks. Violet apologized, sat back, and waited patiently for Pastor Luke to pray so they could eat. The Evanses then bowed their heads, and Violet did the same out of respect even though she wasn't actually praying.

"God, first off, we'd like to thank you for providing us with this food. Second, we'd like to thank you for Violet. She's a beautiful daughter of yours, and we thank you for being able to have her here tonight. In your great name, amen," said Pastor Luke.

The prayer was over, and it was now time to eat, but Violet didn't touch her food for a while. Pastor Luke could tell she was in a deep thought, and he had a strong feeling it was about his prayer. He knew that she wasn't really praying at that time, but at least she was listening.

Violet snapped out of her deep thought and started digging in. "This is really good," she said.

"I agree. My wife's cooking is the best," added Pastor Luke.

There was a short moment of awkward silence, but that was broken quickly by Pastor Luke.

"Violet, tell me a little about yourself."

"I'm in the third grade, math is my favorite subject, and I live with my mom."

"What about your dad?" added Isabella.

"Isabella, that's none of your business," said Mrs. Evans.

"No, it's okay. He's been absent since I was four."

"That's got to be hard," said Mrs. Evans.

Pastor Luke could tell that Violet was uncomfortable, so he quickly changed the subject. "How did you and Isabella meet?"

"I saw her sitting alone in the cafeteria. It looked like she could use a friend, so I joined her," replied Violet.

"It was nice making a friend on my first day at a new school," added Isabella.

"That's so sweet. Looks like you two get along quite well," said Mrs. Evans.

The conversation between the Evans family and Violet went well from that point forward. Mr. and Mrs. Evans told stories about each state they had lived in, what it was like having to travel around a lot, and Isabella's early youth. Violet being at the dinner table with Isabella and her parents made her long for her father. *I have to fix this, and hopefully it works this time,* Violet said to herself as she recalled the photo of her and her family on her fourth birthday. She still wanted to go in there and attempt to stop her father from ever leaving.

Dinner was now over. Violet expressed how appreciative she was for the meal and the family's hospitality. She and Isabella then headed back upstairs. Pastor Luke and Mrs. Evans cleaned up the table, washed the dishes, and talked about how glad they were that Isabella had made her first friend at her new school and that it was Violet. Pastor Luke was worried about Violet, but his worries were about to be put to rest. He had forgotten to let Violet know that her mom would be here to pick her up around eight. He headed upstairs to tell her, but before he entered Isabella's room, he couldn't help but overhear the conversation they were having. It would confirm that what Pastor Luke had been thinking all along was correct.

"Isabella, why did your dad mention that I was a daughter of God?" asked Violet.

"We're all God's children," replied Isabella.

"So God is like my father?"

"God is like *a* father—loving, comforting, and looking after us. We're all God's children, and he cares about all of us."

What Isabella was saying sparked Violet's interest, so she asked a question about what her dad had said to her when they were talking at Sunset Peak. "Do you think he has a plan for all of us?" asked Violet.

"Of course! God has something great out there for us. At times it may not seem like it, but it's there. You just have to be patient and trust him," Isabella responded.

"I have a hard time trusting something that I can't see."

"There were times when I did, too, but I sought God, and he didn't let me down," replied Isabella. "Hey, you should come to church this Sunday. My dad's giving a good message. It's one that you definitely won't want to miss."

"Thanks for the invite, but I don't know. I'll think about it."

"The invite will always be there."

Pastor Luke couldn't have been prouder of his daughter. She was applying what she'd learned in church, and that was to witness to those who were struggling to believe. It was going to take some more convincing, but Pastor Luke was going to put that in God's hands. Before Violet left to go home, he would make the biggest contribution of all. Once Violet and Isabella were done talking, Pastor Luke went in and told Violet that her mom would be there shortly and to make sure that she had all her things together. As Pastor Luke was leaving the room, he couldn't help but turn around and smile at Violet. He knew that God was working in her life already.

Violet and Isabella decided to play Go Fish. Before they knew it, Violet's mom was there. Violet grabbed her stuff, hugged Isabella goodbye, and headed downstairs. Violet went to the family room to say goodbye to Mrs. Evans too and thank her again. Pastor Luke was waiting at the front door to show Violet out.

"It was nice having you over. You're always welcome in the Evans household."

"Thanks. Looking forward to my next visit. Have a good night, Mr. Evans."

"Thanks. You too, Violet."

As Violet walked to her mom's car, Pastor Luke proceeded to say something that stopped her dead in her tracks. "And Violet...one more thing."

"What's that?"

"Just because you're not pursuing God doesn't mean he's not pursuing you."

Huh, thought Violet as she stood there with a blank expression on her face. She didn't understand, but the words stuck with her for the rest of the night.

When she got in the car, her mom asked her how the night had gone, but she didn't respond.

"Everything okay, sweetie?" her mom inquired, but still Violet didn't respond. Her mom assumed she was too tired to talk after a long day at school and her time with Isabella.

Violet was still in deep thought about Pastor Luke's part-ing words.

What did he mean by that? Violet thought to herself. After she thought about what Pastor Luke had said, she still had some-thing else on her mind. It was the shoebox; she wanted to test the picture out again. Violet had a feeling that this time it was going to work. It was one of the last items in the box—it had to work.

"I need to fix this. It's all my fault," Violet thought out loud.

"You need to fix what? What's your fault?" Violet's mom was struck by the statement.

"Seeing Isabella and both of her parents reminds me of what I don't have."

"You still think what happened with your dad is your fault?"

"Yeah, I do. There's so much guilt that I carry with me every day."

"It's not your fault, Violet."

"How can you say that? If it weren't for me, he'd still be here."

Violet's mom kept trying to convince her, but Violet didn't want to listen anymore, and once they pulled into the driveway she ran inside and went to her room right away.

Mrs. Cooper got out of the car and slowly walked inside. Her heart was once again aching for her daughter. She had tried her best to make Violet feel better and it had failed, so that made her feel even worse. Jennifer was also disappointed, because now they might not be able to have their quality time after all. As she made her way up the stairs to head to her room, she could hear Violet crying, so she went into Violet's room in one last attempt to speak with her before she went to her room.

"Violet, I can't tell you how to feel, but I'll be praying. Also, if you need anything, I'm always right down the hallway."

Violet was on her stomach with her head in the pillow and didn't respond, so her mom bent down to give her a hug and a good night kiss on the back of her head. Then she left the room.

Once Violet had calmed down, she couldn't help but think again about what Pastor Luke had said.

Maybe my mom would know the answer to this. Violet got out of her bed and walked down the hallway to her mom's room. She saw that the light was off, so her mom was more than likely asleep. *I don't want to wake her up, but she did say that she'd always be here to talk.* Violet quietly opened the door and entered the room; she went over and lightly tapped her mom on the shoulder to wake her up.

"Mom…Mom…"

Violet's mom was startled, but she was relieved to see that it was her daughter. "Everything okay?"

"I have a question about God," said Violet. "Pastor Luke told me that God pursues us, even when we're not pursuing him. What does that mean?"

"Even though we don't want a relationship with God, he still wants a relationship with us."

Violet was still kind of confused, so she asked her mom to explain it differently.

"You and I have a mother-daughter relationship. Remember the other day when you said that you didn't love me anymore and said that you wanted me to leave you alone? Well, I'll always continue to love you, want to be around you, and be there for you," Mrs. Cooper explained. "The same goes for God. God wants to be a part of your life even if you don't want to be a part of his, and he will always love you, even when you don't love him back."

"Oh okay, I think I get it now." Violet still wanted to spend some time with her mom and hear her mom and dad's love story, so she thought she would ask even though her mom looked tired. The worst she could say is no.

"Hey, Mom, do you think you could tell me the story about you and Dad? Please!"

Jennifer was tired, but again she saw this as another opportunity to spend time with her daughter, so it was hard to turn down.

"Of course! Why don't you crawl up here into bed next to me, and I'll be more than happy to tell you all about it."

Jennifer and Tommy both went to Bentley High School, but they never formally met until that fateful night when Tommy rescued Jennifer and her family from the fire. They lived in two completely different worlds in high school. Tommy hung out with the jocks and was very well liked among his peers, viewed as a natural-born leader, many looked up to him, and by his junior year when he took over as quarterback, he became known as the king of Bentley High. Jennifer, on the other hand, was in a way different crowd. She was a theater kid who was in the drama club, participated in academic events such as the Quiz Bowl, and was on the debate team. She was considered nice, extremely intelligent, and caring. Boys also thought she was stunning but were intimidated by her intellect. The one thing they did have in common is that they were both devout Christians who loved God and helped out in their churches whenever they had the opportunity.

Jennifer had a huge crush on Tommy, but she had always been too afraid to go up and talk to him. She had plenty of opportunities when she passed him in the hallways, shared a couple of classes with him, and when she would go hang out with her friends group at the Old Town Diner after the football games on Friday Night. Even though she had plenty of chances, she would still pass them up, so she admired him from afar.

By the time Jennifer was a senior she struck up enough courage to go up and talk to Tommy, but changed her mind when she embarrassed herself in front of him. One day as she was walking out of the cafeteria, Tommy caught her eye like usual, but she didn't realize the door she was heading toward was closed, and she ran right into it. The whole cafeteria went silent and stared at her. She'd never been so embarrassed in her life and it didn't help that the boy she had a huge crush on was there to witness this. Jennifer took this as a sign that it just wasn't meant to be and moved on.

On the night of the big football game where Tommy pushed his team into the state finals, she had a change of heart. Jennifer decided to stick around, so she could finally go up to Tommy and introduce herself, but there were so many girls waiting for him to get his autograph. Once again, she didn't get the chance to meet him. Jennifer was so discouraged that she didn't bother going out with her friends to the Old Town Diner to celebrate and decided to go home.

Later that night, she was awaken by the smell of smoke and realized that there was a fire in the house. Jennifer tried to escape her room, but it was no use because the heat was so intense by her door. She thought for sure that this was the end, and in desperation she got on her knees and started praying to God that she would make it out alive. Jennifer passed out from the smoke, and a few minutes later, Tommy made it past the fire, busted down her door, and carried her to safety. On the way out of the burning home, she woke up and smiled at Tommy. Tommy smiled back and from that moment on, she had a good feeling that this was the man that God intended for her to marry.

That following Monday, she saw Tommy in the hallway and wanted to thank him for saving her life, but he was in a hurry to get to class. However, on the way to class, Tommy dropped one of his books, and this gave Jennifer a great idea. She picked up the book, but before giving it back to him, she wrote her phone number on a piece of paper and put it in the front of the book. Tommy gave Jennifer a call, and from that day going forward, they were inseparable.

Tommy would pick Jennifer up each morning to go to school; they would hold hands while walking in the hallways, eat lunch together, and spend every moment they could together in between classes. On the weekends, they would head to Sunset Peak and talk for hours about their dreams and aspirations and their love for God. Tommy wanted to get a degree in business and work for a Fortune 500 company, and Jennifer wanted to get a degree in social work and help disadvantaged children. They lived in a small town their entire lives and were thinking bigger, so they always dreamed about going to college in a big city but still wanted to stay somewhere warm.

While they were talking about their big plans for the future, in the back of Tommy's mind, he was thinking how much he wanted Jennifer to be a part of his, so he began coming up with a plan to ask her to marry him. Tommy had arranged for Jennifer to go out on an all-day girls' trip while he sat down with her parents to get their blessing to marry their daughter. Jennifer's parents were thrilled and overly excited because they knew the kind of man Tommy was and that their daughter would be left in good hands.

When Jennifer got home from her girls' trip, she noticed a trail of rose petals leading up the stairs all the way into her bedroom. This was the exact same place where Tommy saved Jennifer's life, and now here he was asking her to spend the rest of their lives together.

When she arrived to her bedroom, there was Tommy standing there in a suit. He got down on one knee and popped the question. Jennifer was overwhelmed by emotions, and her heart was full. The man she fancied for the past four years was now asking her to marry him.

Right after Tommy and Jennifer got married they packed everything up and moved to Orlando, Florida. Once they graduated college, they were expecting their first child, and it was a girl. Tommy and Jennifer were having a hard time coming up with a name, but once in a while Tommy would come home with some violets, and every time he handed them to Jennifer, the baby started kicking. To them, that was a sign that they should name their baby girl Violet.

"That's how your father and I met, fell in love, and came up with your name."

"That's the best love story I've ever heard. Better than the ones in the Disney movies you and I used to watch."

"It was a magical time in my life. I hope you get to experience the same thing one day."

"This could be something that I include in my story. Add some romance to it."

Violet had just opened the door for Jennifer to ask her about the story. She was really curious about the shoebox Violet found and why this story was so important to her. Maybe Violet was trying to get something out of it. It could possibly be getting her to think about her dad and opening up more in her sessions with Mrs. Turner.

"Mrs. Turner told me that you found a shoebox with some items that Dad left behind. Could you show me? I've never seen them before."

"I didn't actually find a shoebox. The shoebox is just an idea that I added to my story."

"Oh, okay...is there something that you hope to get out of this story? There has to be a reason why you're doing it."

"My hope is that I'll be able to bring Dad back."

"Wait...what?"

"I said I'm going to bring Dad back."

"Violet...a story isn't going to change anything. You can't bring your father back to life."

"You can try..."

"But, Violet—"

"Mom, I don't want to hear anything else. I'm going back to my room."

Jennifer was now extremely frightened for her daughter's mental well-being. It all made sense to her now as to why she hung out alone all the time. Violet had created this fictitious world through her story where her father was alive so she no longer had to deal with one where he was dead.

This morning when I heard her running around...she must've been imaginary playing with her father. Running around like they used to in our backyard before he died, thought Jennifer.

Violet went back into her room and started pacing back and forth.

Who is my mom to tell me what I can and can't do? She doesn't know anything, thought Violet. She was right about one thing; her mom didn't know that this just wasn't some story. That the shoebox, the items it contained and Violet being able to see her father, were, in fact, real. However, there was no guarantee that she'd be able to bring her father back. All she could do now was try.

Violet then remembered what her mom said about God still loving her and wanting to be a part of her life even if she didn't want the same. Violet came up with an idea and wanted to put that theory to the test.

"Okay, God, if you're really there and do love me, then I'll be able to go into the picture and stop my dad from ever leaving."

Violet left her room to head up to the attic once again. When she got up there, she made her way to the shoebox one more time. Violet opened it, and there was the picture.

"Here it is, God," said Violet, but nothing happened with the photo. "What are you waiting for?"

Still nothing.

"Guess I was right after all."

Violet placed the photo back in the shoebox and started to leave the attic.

Ten

Once again, the picture looked like it wasn't going to work. Violet was so sure that this time was going to be different. A plan that was once so promising now seemed like a lost cause. She might just have to accept the fact that her father wasn't coming back after all. Violet was now all out of ideas, and the only thing left she could do was go to bed.

Violet approached the attic stairs and saw a light at the bottom. She stopped because she thought it was her mom. After waiting awhile and hearing no footsteps coming toward her, she made her way down the stairs. There wasn't any light on; it was actually the sun shining through the window because it was daytime.

I couldn't have been in there that long? thought Violet. She returned to her room, but it wasn't the same. There were her toys from when she was a toddler, along with her old My Little Pony comforter and the kitchen set she used to have.

No way, thought Violet. Her suspicions were about to be proven right. When she looked at the calendar in her room, there it was: March 26, 2016.

It worked; it actually worked, thought Violet. Here was Violet's chance to redo the past and get her family back. *I have to sneak around, though. Even though I'm in my own house, I'm now a stranger.*

Violet made her way to the stairs and looked down to see whether the coast was clear. There was no one in sight because they were all outside in the backyard that day, so Violet moved quickly and went into the kitchen. When she got into the kitchen, she saw a man approaching the door; it was her Uncle Steve. Violet was about to leave the kitchen and go into the family room, but she heard someone else coming from that direction, so she had to hide in the kitchen pantry.

That was close, thought Violet as she waited for her Uncle Steve to head back outside. The coast was clear again, so she exited the pantry and headed to the window by the kitchen sink to get a better look outside.

Outside were her family and friends; she even saw her younger self.

I look so happy.

What she saw next brought her to tears. Her father walked over to her younger self and picked her up to hold her in his arms.

I miss those times, thought Violet. Everything was going in the right direction in Violet's present life: she had a good friend in Isabella, made a lot of progress in her sessions with Mrs. Turner, things were starting to get better between her and her mom and she was doing better in the classroom. Yet still, Violet felt empty inside because of the absence of her dad.

The water balloon fight between her friends had finished, which meant that it was almost time to open presents.

My father will be leaving to get my present soon. I have to find a place to wait by the front door so I can stop him.

There was a hallway that led to the laundry room by the front door, so Violet would go there and wait. Violet looked around the corner, and there was her mom—a younger version of her mom—walking upstairs to change younger Violet into some new clothes. Right behind her was her father making his way to the door.

There's my dad. Here's my last chance. As Violet started making her way to the front door, she felt a pull on her arm.

"Let go of me," cried Violet. She tried to pull away, but the grip remained. "I said *let go.*"

"Violet, calm down. It's me," said the voice. Violet turned around and right before her very eyes was her dad.

"Dad, you have to let go. I have to stop you from leaving."

"Violet, you can't—"

Violet interrupted to plead with him again. "Once you leave, you don't come back. Let me make this right. We can be a family again—you, Mom, and me."

Violet's dad tried reasoning with her once more but was interrupted again.

"It's my fault. I did this to you. Let me undo this," Violet was still pleading.

"Violet, you can't undo what's already been done…I'm dead."

"Don't say that! It's all because of me you're dead. I'm supposed to fix this!" yelled Violet.

"No, it's not."

"It's not?"

"No, but come with me and I'll explain everything."

Violet's dad reached out his hand and told Violet to take it, but she was scared. Violet was so sure that the whole purpose of this journey had been to save her dad. She was clueless as to what any of this meant anymore, so she was unsure about whether she wanted to go with him.

"You trust me, don't you?" asked Violet's dad.

"I just thought the whole point of finding this shoebox was to be able to bring you back. What's the point of going with you now?"

"Come with me, and I'll tell you everything. You have to trust me, though."

"You pinky promise?" asked Violet as she put her pinky out toward her dad.

Violet's dad extended his pinky and promised her that everything would be okay. Violet took her dad's hand, he counted to three, and then a warm, comforting light blinded Violet. Once the blinding light was gone, and she could see again, Violet couldn't believe where she was.

"What is this place?"

"Some people call it heaven, but for me it's home."

She saw a big blue sky, fluffy white clouds, green pastures with animals roaming around, streams of water, gardens with flowers and vegetables, and a giant radiant sun shining down that made everything look golden. There were also houses, farms, beaches, and parks. Children were running around playing with their families; other families were hanging out in their front yards enjoying the scenery; some were swimming in the streams, and others were with their pets in the pastures. It was a utopia, the likes of which Violet had never imagined. Everyone looked so young, alive, and happy to be there. Violet did notice that there were some people hanging out by themselves and was confused.

"There are families, but some are here by themselves. Why?"

"Just like me, they're waiting for their family members to cross over into the afterlife, so they can be reunited."

"Aren't you all sad and missing everybody?"

"Missing everyone, yes, but there is no such thing as sad here. Take a look around. What do you notice about everyone?"

"Everyone looks happy, healthy, free, and alive."

"That's heaven for you: no more pain, no more suffering, and no more tears. There's only peace, joy, and love here. Now I have a couple of special people I'd like you to meet."

Violet and her dad followed the black path, which was the way to get around the community. It led to their first stop. They came up to a blue house with a white picket fence and a big garden.

"Who lives here?" asked Violet.

Mr. Cooper told her to be patient, that it was a surprise. Violet was in shock when she saw who came to the door: it was Lucy and Mark, who had taken care of her during her first journey.

"What's going on? I don't understand," said Violet.

"These were my guardian angels when I was alive," replied Violet's dad.

"What's that?"

"Guardian angels watch over us and protect us."

"They're *your* guardian angels, though. I still don't understand."

"When your father died, he made us promise him that we would look after you when the time was right," said Mark and Lucy.

"Time was right?" queried Violet.

Lucy and Mark told Violet that during a person's greatest time of need, God presented him or her with a guardian angel for protection. Lucy and Mark were presented to Violet's dad when his own father died about three years later after going into the hospital due to a heart condition. Violet's dad ended up having the same affliction. That's why he couldn't play football anymore. He knew that he would more than likely meet the same fate, so he put together the shoebox for Violet to find one day.

God knew that this was going to be the most difficult journey of Violet's life, so he let Lucy and Mark fulfill their promise and look after her along the way.

"You all did this for me?" asked Violet.

"You have to give the credit to God. He's the one who set this all up and has been looking out for you this entire time," said Lucy and Mark.

"Violet, think about it—the glimmers of light, dream about the shoebox, Isabella, everyone working to help you. God has been trying to point you in the right direction," said Mr. Cooper.

Violet was trying to listen but was in a daze. She was too busy thinking about one bit of information that Lucy and Mark had told her: "He knew that he would more than likely meet the same fate."

Did he really know he was going to die young? thought Violet. Her dad then suggested that they better get going. He had another surprise along the way, and this time it was to see a really good friend.

Violet and her dad kept walking down the black path until they got to a bridge that looked like a rainbow.

"This bridge—it's so colorful," said Violet.

"Welcome to Rainbow Bridge," her dad responded.

"What's Rainbow Bridge?"

Tommy explained that Rainbow Bridge was a place where pets went in the afterlife while waiting for their owners to cross over.

"That could only mean one thing," said Violet.

Violet's dad told her to whistle, and once she had, Buster came running toward her. Violet was so happy to see her childhood dog, and the feeling was mutual. Buster tackled Violet and proceeded to smother her with kisses.

"I missed you so much, boy," said Violet.

For the time being, Violet was reunited with a companion who had brought her so much joy, and she couldn't have been happier.

"I heard stories about this place but didn't think it was real," said Violet.

"God has a special place for pet's too," replied Mr. Cooper.

"How come there are other pets with their owners, but Buster has no one?" asked Violet.

"Buster's owner hasn't crossed over, so he'll wait here till that day comes."

"If you're not his owner, then who's the owner?"

"Well, you are. Your mom and I were looking at rescue dogs at the shelter a couple days before your fourth birthday and arranged for me to pick up Buster on the day of your party."

Violet's dad insisted they keep on going, but sadly, they had to leave Buster behind. Buster couldn't completely cross the rainbow until Violet came back for good. She got on one knee and held Buster close to her one last time.

"Until we meet again. You were such a good dog. I'm glad you have a forever home. Love you, Bus."

Violet let go of Buster, and off he went back across Rainbow Bridge with all the other pets waiting for their owners. This was a telling sign that eventually Violet was going to have to leave her dad behind too. But for the time being she wanted to enjoy his company.

Violet and her dad went into the field where all the children were playing, and a little girl ran up to Violet and gave her a giant hug. Violet didn't understand why this little girl was drawn to her. She had never met her before.

"You must be Violet," said the little girl.

"Who are you, and how do you know me?" responded Violet.

"My name's Skye, and I was once Isabella's best friend."

Violet didn't know this about Isabella. So Isabella was keeping a secret too. "What happened?" she asked.

Skye told Violet that she and Isabella had both been cancer patients at a children's hospital and had become best friends along the way. Skye didn't believe in God and was angry with the cards she'd been dealt, but seeing Isabella's unshaken faith had inspired her, so she had started asking questions.

"Isabella helped me find God. She saved my life," said Skye.

Isabella was trying to help Violet find God as well, but Violet was having an extremely hard time letting him in.

"I try to visit her in her dreams every once in a while. Please tell her I hope she's doing well and thank her for everything," said Skye. "And Violet, believe it or not, she needs you just as much as you need her. God intended on you two becoming friends."

Violet promised Skye that the next time she saw Isabella she would pass along the message and continued on with her father.

"We have a full day ahead of us. What would you like to do next?" asked Mr. Cooper. Violet looked up at her father with a big grin on her face and said, "You're it."

She tagged her dad, and off they went up and down the fields until they couldn't run anymore. After that, Violet's dad took her to the stream to go fishing. It was her first time fishing, but her dad was more than happy to teach her. This also gave them some time to talk more.

"How's your mom doing?" Her dad knew exactly how her mom was doing but wanted to see if Violet would tell the truth about their relationship.

"She's doing pretty well. We don't really bond that much, though," replied Violet.

Part of Violet's answer was the truth. Violet and her mom never really did bond that often, but Jennifer was, in fact, hurting on the inside. She just couldn't show it because she knew she had to be strong for her daughter.

"She's not doing well, Violet. She's feeling just as torn up about me being gone as you are. When you marry someone, you're marrying your other half, your best friend. I was someone that she could lean on. Now she needs you," her dad explained.

Violet didn't know what to say, but she started feeling bad because she never really did take into account how her mom was feeling.

"Dad, I'm so selfish."

"No, you're not. I'm just trying to open your eyes so you'll take it easy on her. She loves you dearly and is trying to do the best she can for you."

Violet took her father's words seriously. He was right: her mom was only trying to show Violet love the best way she could.

When Violet and her dad were done fishing, they took a long bike ride along the path and made a stop at a farm along the way. Violet saw a bunch of sheep and wanted to go pet them, so Violet and her dad got off their bikes and walked toward the farm. As they were petting the sheep, a man approached them and asked if he could help them. Violet was curious about who this man was and why he had all these sheep.

"I'm a shepherd, but I also love to tell stories," said the man.

"Can you tell my dad and me a story then?" asked Violet.

"It would be my pleasure. This one is the parable about the lost sheep. God is the shepherd, and we are the sheep. A shepherd has one hundred sheep and loses one. Should the shepherd leave the ninety-nine sheep and go search for the one that is lost? Yes, he should, and I'll tell you, when that one sheep is found, he's happier with the one who wandered than he is with the ninety-nine that didn't."

"What's the meaning of that story?" said Violet.

"He's talking about how much love and compassion God has for his people. He values one person no more and no less than every other person," offered her dad.

The shepherd nodded and smiled at Violet's dad because Mr. Cooper was right. He then continued narrating the parable to Violet. "God loves and cares for us so much that even when we wander away from him, he comes after us until we are found once more. God isn't mad; he's rejoicing."

What Pastor Luke and Violet's mom had told her now really clicked. *God left others behind just to come and look for me, even after I walked away from him. Yet I still have trouble believing, and I'm angry with God.*

"I have some more sheep to attend to. You both take care," said the man.

Violet and her father finished visiting the farm and got back on their bikes. Violet's dad told her that this trail led to a hill where you get a nice view of everything. It was a nice place to relax too. This would also be their last stop, after which it would be time for Violet to go home. After their talk, her dad had an even bigger surprise for Violet to end their perfect day together. It was also going to provide further closure and healing, which was going to help her open up even more.

Violet and her dad walked up to the top of a hill, where there was an amazing view of not only the sun, but also the entire community. Mr. Cooper pulled out a blanket for them to sit on so they could relax while they talked. He pulled his daughter close to him, and not a word was said. Violet was too busy taking it all in. She was once again in the loving arms of her father. This was something Violet thought of every night before she went to sleep and could typically only dream of.

Now it was actually happening. After another few moments of silence, Violet's dad spoke. He had so much to explain to Violet before it was time to leave.

"It's not your fault, Violet. It wouldn't have mattered whether or not I left that day."

When Violet's dad left to go get Buster at the rescue shelter that day, he lost control of the car on the way there and ran through a red light into oncoming traffic. He was pronounced dead at the scene. Violet had felt guilty and responsible for her dad's death all those years. She was convinced that if her dad hadn't left, he'd still be alive. It wasn't the crash that killed him. His heart had suddenly stopped while he was behind the wheel.

"I don't know what to say…I've been haunted by guilt all these years. I guess I can say I'm relieved that it wasn't my fault."

"Violet, even if my heart didn't stop and I still got into a car crash and died, it still wouldn't have been your fault. When it's your time…it's your time."

"Did you know that there was a high chance that you could die at a young age?" asked Violet.

"Yeah. I came to learn that my father's heart disease was genetic," replied Violet's dad.

"Yet you continued to live your life to the fullest. How?"

"I had made a promise to my dad, your grandfather."

"What was that?"

"I'd be braver than I believed, stronger than I seemed, smarter than I thought, and that I would keep my faith."

Violet's dad wanted her to promise him the same thing. This journey had helped Violet make tremendous strides, but it was only the beginning. This was a promise to always be these things in life—to always be brave and never think twice about taking chances in life. Violet had learned to be brave after her second journey was over. She was truthful with Isabella and started putting herself out there more, but she missed the most important part. Violet needed to be brave in order to talk about her trauma and come to accept that her father was gone. She had opened up a bit, but she needed to do it willingly. Second was to always be strong and push through the tough times in life. Violet's dad also needed her to be strong for her mom because she was still going through a rough time and needed her daughter more than ever. Lastly, Violet's dad complimented her on her intelligence, encouraging her to always remember how smart she was, to never doubt herself, and to use the brain that God had given her to fulfill her potential.

"Let's reflect on your journey. What do you see?"

Violet was thinking about all the places she'd been, experiences she'd gone through, and progress she'd made; she noticed that these qualities had been in her all along. Violet just needed a push in order to look inside herself and have these qualities woken up.

"Mrs. Turner was right. I did have a lot to offer, but I just never saw this until now. This journey has taught me so much about myself."

The other thing that Violet saw in herself was a sense of emptiness.

Right now when I'm with my dad, I feel complete and all my pain is gone, but even the thought of being separated again brings everything back, thought Violet. She couldn't stay with her dad forever. She had to find something more to lean on, something that would provide true healing in her. Yes, she had her mom, Isabella, and her support group at school, but that could only do so much. Violet needed something that she could turn to when all hope seemed lost, when she had questions that no one else could answer—something that might fully restore her broken heart.

Violet reflected once more on her journey. It all was now making sense. God was the one thing that her dad, mom, and good friend Isabella turned to when they were going through their own struggles in life. When her grandfather had been sick and eventually died, her dad turned to God. When Isabella was in the hospital with cancer and her best friend Skye died, she turned to God. Her mom was in pain and unsure what would happen with Violet, but she continued to turn to God. Violet had been so angry this entire time that she kept on missing it. After hearing what God had done and how much he really loved her, she started feeling convinced. Violet had a feeling about what she had to do, but the question was how. Looking toward and trusting in something that you couldn't even see could be scary, and that's exactly what Violet was feeling. This was the last promise that Violet's dad needed her to fulfill.

Before Violet could get out another word, her dad told her that it was getting late and that it was time for her to go home. Violet started looking sad and clung onto her dad and didn't want to let go.

"I don't want to go. There's one more question that I need answered."

"Don't worry, you can ask me while I'm tucking you in one last time."

"I want to stay just a little longer. Please!"

"Let's get you home, Violet. Don't want Mom to notice you're missing and then have her worried sick about you."

As before, Violet's dad told her to take his hand. They counted to three, and before Violet knew it, they were back in the attic of her house.

Mr. Cooper picked Violet up in his arms and went downstairs toward her room. When they got to her room, Violet's dad laid her down, pulled the covers over her, and started to walk toward the bookshelf. He was looking for the Dr. Seuss book he had put there so he could read it to her just like in old times.

"Where is the book I put there, Violet?"

"You put the book there?"

"Yeah, I check in on your mom at times and on you as well. I like to leave reminders that I'm always with you."

Violet felt bad that she had put it under her bed and didn't want to say so, so she pointed to where it was. Violet's dad grabbed the book from underneath the bed and pulled up a chair, but before reading it, he wanted to know why it was there; Dr. Seuss's *One Fish, Two Fish, Red Fish, Blue Fish* had been her favorite book by the author.

"It reminded me of how much pain I was in. That you were gone," explained Violet.

"Think about the good times," her father responded.

He went on to read her the Dr. Seuss book. Before Violet knew it, the story was over, and it was time for her father to go. He put the book back on the shelf and sat on her bed. He tucked her in once more to make sure she was warm, then bent over to give her a good night kiss on the forehead.

"Goodnight, princess, I love you so much. More than you'll ever know. Remember to always be there for your mom. You two need each other more than ever."

"Goodbye and good night. I love you too, Daddy. I'll miss you, and don't worry; I'll be there for her just like she's been there for me."

"I'll miss you, too, but whenever you do miss me, look down at your heart. I'll always be in there."

Her father started to get up from the bed, but Violet grabbed onto his arm. She wasn't ready for him to go yet. She still needed one last question answered. Violet's father couldn't have answered her questions more perfectly. All the doubts that Violet had been having about God lately were all about to be put to rest.

"Daddy, I want to believe, but how do I let him in?"

"You have to let go and let God."

"What do you mean?"

"Any fear, anger, sadness, doubts you've held onto in your heart you need to let go of. You can't let your heart be blinded by those things. You have to open up your heart more than ever and let him in."

"But I'm scared Daddy."

"I get that it can be scary reaching for something that isn't physically there, but you have to reach out by faith and hold onto that. Trust in God wholeheartedly, and he will take care of you."

"You pinky promise?"

"I promise, because the more I trusted in God and put my life in his hands, the more I understood that he has promises for us, too, and they became true."

"I'll try. I really will."

"I have to go now. Tell your mom I said hi. Love you, princess."

"Are you sure you can't stay?"

"Violet, I don't belong here anymore. My time has come and gone, but yours is about to truly begin. You just have to accept the help that's been in front of you all along."

"Goodbye, Daddy. I love you too."

"It's not 'goodbye.' It's 'I'll see you again.'"

Violet's dad started walking away from her bed. There was another huge flash of light, and just like that, he was gone. Violet was sad at first because her time with her dad was over, but she decided she was going to be positive.

Don't be sad that it's over; be happy that it happened, thought Violet. This was something that her mother always tried to tell her. Violet rolled over on her side, and there was the Dr. Seuss book that her dad had put back on the shelf. Violet couldn't help but smile at it. Her dad had read it to her one last time, and this would be a memory that Violet would cherish forever. Violet got out of bed to go get the book, crawled back into bed, and held it closely to her. But before she fell asleep, she looked up and said, "Okay, God, I'm listening. What's next?"

Then she closed her eyes and fell into a deep sleep.

Eleven

"Violet! Violet!" a strange voice called out. Violet woke up, but she wasn't in her room; she was near a lake. The voice called out to her once more, "Violet! Violet!"

She didn't know where it was coming from. All she could see in front of her was fog and a lot of water.

Where's that voice coming from? she thought.

"Violet, follow my voice." Violet followed the voice and kept going forward until she had reached the edge of the lake.

Violet didn't want to go any further. It sounded like the voice was calling from way out there, and Violet didn't have a boat or anything else to get to it.

"If I go any further, I'll be underwater," Violet called out to the voice.

"You can walk to me."

"How can I walk to you? I'll sink, and I won't be able to breathe."

The voice told her that she had to believe and shouldn't worry. The voice then told Violet that not one drop of water would get on her clothes. Violet couldn't believe what she was hearing. The idea of getting in the water and not ending up wet seemed impossible.

"Violet, just put your feet out one at a time and come toward me."

All right, here goes nothing, Violet thought to herself. She closed her eyes and started to walk forward.

"Violet, open your eyes."

Violet opened her eyes and was in shock. She hadn't sunk even though she was above the water. She looked down and could see fish swimming underneath her feet, all the way to the bottom of the lake.

This is so cool, thought Violet.

"Now walk toward me."

Violet continued to walk toward the voice; the person who was now in front of her she had seen before. It was the shepherd who had told her the parable of the lost sheep.

"I've seen you before. I know you," said Violet.

"My father and I have known you before you were even born. We also know your heart and exactly what you need," said the shepherd. "Walk forward a little more. He's waiting for you."

"Who's waiting for me?"

"My father."

Violet started walking forward and was hit by an overwhelming sense of peace. There was a flash of light—it was so warm and comforting to Violet. She wanted to walk closer to it, but then she heard, "Stop." Violet came to a complete standstill, and out of the light appeared a hand.

Another strange voice called out to Violet. "It's time, Violet. Take my hand."

As Violet was reaching out her hand, she heard a loud knock and another voice. "Violet…Violet…Violet…"

She awoke from her dream. It was her mom telling her that it was time to get up and get ready for school. Violet didn't know what to make of the dream.

What did the person mean by "It's time"? thought Violet. The dream didn't make sense to her, but it felt so real. *I'll have to ask Isabella about this one.* Violet hurried up and got ready because she had something important to say to her mom. Something that'd been long overdue.

Violet got her stuff together for the day and ran downstairs. Her mom was in the kitchen making pancakes for breakfast and was surprised by Violet's good morning hug.

"You haven't done that since you were little."

Violet kept holding on and didn't want to let go. Her mom tried to pull away, but Violet only kept squeezing more tightly.

"Honey, I love you, too, but I have to finish making breakfast."

"I don't want to let go. I love you, Mom, and I'm sorry."

Violet explained that she was sorry for the way she'd been treating her mom over the years. After the talk with her dad, she had come to realize that her mom was only trying to show her how much she loved and cared for her.

"Mom, I want to go back to the way things used to be between us."

"I would love that, sweetie. We don't really talk or bond that often anymore."

Violet knew exactly where to start, and she knew that this was going to make her mom very happy.

"You want to possibly go to church this Sunday?"

"*You* want to go to church?"

"I'm still thinking about it. Isabella invited me to her church, and I thought it would be nice if we went together."

Violet's mom didn't know what to say. One moment, Violet didn't even want to believe in God, and the next, she was thinking about going back to church. But Mrs. Cooper also knew not to question God.

"You know I would definitely love to go, but let me know what you decide," replied Violet's mom. "Happy Fri-yay by the way."

Violet and her mom had a really nice breakfast, for a change, to start the morning. They were enjoying each other's company so much that they lost track of time, and Violet was about to be late for school.

"I have another meeting today at school with everyone, so just wait in the office for me until the meeting is over," said Violet's mom.

Violet grabbed her stuff, got in the car with her mom, and off they went to school. Violet was hoping she would get there before all the kids went into their classrooms so she could have a word with Isabella about the dream she had. Isabella might be able to clear up the questions she had about her dream.

Violet's mom pulled up to school, and Violet noticed that there weren't any kids waiting outside to be let in, an indication that she was late.

If I hurry, I can catch Isabella in the hallways before she heads into her classroom. Violet grabbed her backpack, said goodbye to her mom, and quickly got out of the car.

Violet took off running in an effort to catch up with Isabella before class started. When she got inside, she saw that there weren't any students in the hallway. *Maybe I'll run into her on the way to my classroom*, thought Violet, but as she went by Isabella's classroom, she saw that Isabella was in her seat doing her morning reading. Violet was going to have to wait, but she couldn't. A desire to know the meaning of the dream right away was weighing on her heart.

Violet quietly said, "Isabella...hey...over here."

But Isabella didn't respond. Violet tried the same approach a second time, and still nothing.

How am I going to get her attention? thought Violet. Violet had no choice left but to knock on the door and ask the teacher if Isabella could step out into the hallway to discuss something important.

The teacher told Isabella that she had five minutes and to hurry up because they were about to meet at the carpet for their daily morning meeting.

"Isabella, I had this dream last night, and I thought maybe you'd know what it meant," Violet began.

"I can try my best. What was the dream about?" Isabella responded.

Violet told Isabella that she had woken up by a lake and kept hearing someone call her name, that she didn't know who it was at first. They were telling her to step onto the water and trust that she wouldn't sink, so she did and was walking on water. Then before she knew it, there was this big flash of light and a strange voice told her that it was time, to take his hand.

"Violet, that's a dream straight from God," said Isabella.

"Really?" asked Violet.

Isabella explained to Violet that God was calling her to step out of her comfort zone and do something that she'd never done before, to release all her doubts and walk with him.

"Are you sure that's what it meant?" Violet responded.

"I've heard my dad preach about it before at church multiple times. I'm positive."

Isabella was about to walk back into class, but Violet wanted to stop her because she wanted to keep the promise she had made to Skye.

"Isabella, wait," said Violet.

"I have to go back in the classroom," Isabella explained as she was walking away.

"It's about Skye," Violet responded.

Isabella stopped walking. An image of her final moments with her best friend appeared in her mind, and she placed her hand over her heart. She hadn't heard that name for quite some time.

"How do you know that name?"

"It's complicated to explain."

"Meet me outside after school, and we can talk more."

Isabella didn't say a word and walked back into her classroom. Violet did the same but felt bad because she could tell that Isabella was hurt by the mere sound of Skye's name.

Violet got to class late, but Mrs. Summers was still really happy to see her.

"Glad you could join us today," she said.

"Glad I'm here too," replied Violet, as she went to go put her stuff away.

Mrs. Summers reminded her that she still needed to go see Mrs. Turner for her usual morning session and encouraged her to get a move on. As Violet was heading out the door, Mrs. Summers offered another folded note for her to give to Mrs.

Turner. Mrs. Summers smiled at Violet. Violet smiled back, and off she went into the hallway toward Mrs. Turner's office.

Violet wasn't disappointed this time to go see Mrs. Turner. She had experienced a lot since Tuesday and had a lot to share with her. Mrs. Turner was more than likely going to ask about how her story was going since she told Violet that they would talk about it next time. Violet had reached a conclusion in her story and was more than prepared to share it. She was learning to come to terms with this conclusion, and it was going to help her with moving forward in life.

Violet didn't even knock this time. She just went into Mrs. Turner's office, handed her the note, and took a seat because she wanted to get down to business. Mrs. Turner opened the note: "Shared story with class yesterday. Ask her about it."

Mrs. Turner started to talk about the note that Mrs. Summers had given her and asked how Violet's story was going, but Violet cut her off before she could get another word out.

"He's dead," said Violet.

Mrs. Turner knew Violet was admitting this with a heavy heart but was also happy because this meant she had come to the final stage of grieving, which was acceptance and now ready to truly move forward.

"You reached the end of your story?" asked Mrs. Turner.

"Yeah, my father's dead, and he's never coming back," replied Violet.

"Is there anything good that came out of this story?"

"I'm not feeling guilty anymore about my father's death. I finally have closure with my father."

"Is there anything else?"

"I saw that my father was the bravest, most selfless, thoughtful human being ever. He knew that he more than likely had little time left on earth but still lived his life with purpose and always put others before himself. I...I...want to be just like him."

"Violet, I know this must be really hard. It's never easy accepting the loss of a loved one, but you've been so strong, and I couldn't be prouder of you."

"You really mean that?"

"Yes. We've been working at this for the past couple of years. Before this point, you wouldn't even talk, and when you did you'd be in denial about your father," replied Mrs. Turner.

"Now that you've come to terms with your father's death, the healing process can begin. I'm really excited for our future sessions."

"What's the next step to moving forward?"

"The first way we could move forward next session is if we walk through what happened the day your father died and talk about how you felt. Just because you've come to acceptance doesn't mean the pain or trauma of the loss is gone. Do you feel ready?"

"I'm finally ready now. Talking my problems out and expressing how I feel is the only way that things are going to get better."

Even though their session had just started, Mrs. Turner knew that this would be enough for today. She was quite pleased with Violet's progress, and this was going to be good news to share with everyone else in the meeting this afternoon. Before Violet left, Mrs. Turner offered her some candy out of the jar on her desk, and Violet was more than happy to take some. Violet then gave Mrs. Turner a giant hug and proceeded to go back to class. She usually had her head down after sessions with Mrs. Turner, but she was sure walking tall today, with a pleasant smile too.

"Violet, you're looking pretty chipper today. Glad to see you're in a good mood," commented Principal Stevens.

"Thanks, Mr. Stevens, and happy Fri-yay."

Violet went on to have her best day yet at school. She participated in everything—raised her hand to read out loud, went up to the board to solve some math problems, and helped Mrs. Summers pass out school supplies. To Mrs. Summers's great delight, the other students even asked Violet to review their stories during the writers' workshop. Violet was becoming the pupil that Mrs. Summers always believed she could be.

Before going to her meeting, Mrs. Summers wanted to talk with Violet about her day and tell her how proud she was of her for stepping up during these past couple of days. Mrs. Summers got up to walk into the hallway and motioned for Violet to come out there as well.

"Am I in trouble?" asked Violet.

"No, silly, I just wanted to talk with you about your progress in class."

Mrs. Summers told Violet that her improvements were really inspiring. They were a sign that there were greater things to come for Violet academically. Mrs. Summers was looking forward to seeing how Violet would do with the two years she had left before moving on to middle school. Yet she had one more thing to tell Violet, which was going to be the best news yet.

"Thanks, Mrs. Summers, for always believing in me. I wish you could be my teacher forever."

"How would you like for me to be your teacher next year?"

"But how?"

Mrs. Summers was getting moved to the fourth-grade classroom and had already asked Principal Stevens if she could retain Violet and have her in her classroom next year.

"I'm so happy right now. I can't wait to tell my mom," said Violet.

She ran back into the classroom and continued to talk with her classmates while she had her afternoon snack. Mrs. Summers couldn't have been prouder of Violet. The success that Violet was finally displaying in the classroom gave her teacher high hopes for Violet's future. Also the students who were once afraid of her were now gravitating toward her and asking her for advice. Mrs. Summers looked down at her watch and saw that she was going to be late for the meeting, so she hurried to the principal's office.

She arrived in Principal Stevens's conference room. There was a different vibe in the room this time. Their meeting on Tuesday following the incident that day had been more serious, and everyone hoped that the plan they had conceived for Violet going forward was going to work. This time, though, everyone looked at ease because of what they had witnessed over the last four days. Today's meeting was going to be nothing but good news and recognition of everyone playing their part in helping Violet.

"Glad to have you all here this afternoon. We're here to discuss Violet's progress with Mrs. Turner, in the classroom with Mrs. Summers, and with Mrs. Cooper at home," said Principal Stevens.

"Violet has shown so much improvement in the classroom. It's night and day compared to how everything was at the beginning of the year. She's participating in class and even socializing with her peers. I have high hopes for her moving forward," exclaimed Mrs. Summers.

"Over the course of the last two years, Violet has barely spoken to me, and when she did, it was obvious that she was dodging the real reason why she was even here in the first place. Let me explain how this all played out," Mrs. Turner added.

She went into an explanation of Violet's story about her father. Mrs. Turner had allowed her to continue to write because the story was about her father who she'd been refusing to talk about over the years. Mrs. Turner had seen children in the past that had experienced the loss of a loved one and would make a story to help them come to terms with their death. Her hope was that she would get the same results with Violet. Mrs. Turner's predictions had been proven correct, of course, by the content of her meeting with Violet that morning.

"Now that she's no longer in denial, we can help her come to terms with her realization so she can move forward and live a healthy life. We can go forward in our sessions with coping techniques and dealing with the grief and hurt from the loss she has left," said Mrs. Turner.

"I have a question. Why did it take so long for Violet to get past the denial stage of grieving?" asked Mrs. Cooper.

"Well, everyone grieves differently. She experienced great loss at the age of four. From the age of three to six, children see death as temporary and reversible. For example, she waited at the bottom of the stairs each night for her father to come home. Also, she's still dealing with trauma, and kids who deal with trauma develop at a slower rate than kids who don't. Kids at the age of six to eight start to get a better grip on the concept of death. Maybe Violet wasn't emotionally ready to understand," replied Mrs. Turner.

"Would guilt have anything to do with it? She mentioned to me the other night that she needed to fix this and felt like the death of her father was her fault."

"Guilt had a lot to do with it as well. Violet's father left to go get her present, and he died on the way. In Violet's mind, if it weren't for her, then her father would be alive. She denied and suppressed memories so she didn't have to feel that guilt."

"How are things going at home, by the way?" asked Principal Stevens.

"She's opening up to me more, and we're actually spending some quality time together. Before, she wouldn't say a word to me at dinner or only goodbye in the morning. She would also spend a lot of time in her room," explained Mrs. Cooper.

"I experienced the same thing in class. Violet would barely participate, barely say good morning to me or talk with her classmates. I would try to engage with her, but she would push me away," added Mrs. Summers.

"I did as well. It took a lot for her to talk about some of the things she did in our sessions, but here's the thing we have to realize: Violet was, and more than likely still is, in a very fragile stage. Dealing with the death of a parent is never easy. Children who have dealt with this type of situation tend to self-isolate, have a hard time expressing themselves and being close with others," said Mrs. Turner.

"What's the plan moving forward?" asked Mrs. Cooper.

Now that Violet was no longer in denial, the plan was to continue with the morning sessions with Mrs. Turner so Violet could open up more about how she was feeling and work on coping techniques. As Violet continued to show signs of improvement, they would cut back on the sessions, and eventually Violet wouldn't have to see Mrs. Turner anymore (though she was always more than welcome to pop into the office).

Mrs. Summers broke the good news to Mrs. Cooper that she was going to teach fourth grade and had already requested that Violet be in her class. Mrs. Cooper was overjoyed because Mrs. Summers was everything a teacher should be—loving, caring, encouraging, and understanding. She knew her daughter would be in good hands during the fourth grade. Mrs. Turner then suggested that Violet should have a productive summer, that perhaps she could go to a summer camp. She also wanted to continue her sessions over the summer with Violet.

"I'm so thankful for each and every single one of you. Your constant dedication has helped Violet so much," said Mrs. Cooper.

"We're thankful for Violet. She's a really special girl, and we're glad that she's a part of this school," said Principal Stevens.

The meeting was over, and the dismissal bell had rung. Violet headed down to the office to meet up with her mom and was really excited to tell her the good news about Mrs.

Summers. When Violet saw her mom, Mrs. Cooper had a pleasant look on her face, which meant that the meeting had gone really well.

"Mom, guess what?" said Violet.

"Let me guess...Mrs. Summers is going to be your teacher next year," replied her mother.

"Yeah, she's the best teacher in the whole wide world."

As Violet and her mom were about to walk out the door, Mrs. Summers stopped them, as she had one more thing to say.

"Violet, I think you're an amazing writer and should continue. Who knows, maybe you'll write children's books like me one day?"

Violet was still shy when it came to compliments, so she hid behind her mom. So Mrs. Cooper mouthed the words "thank you" to her, and off they went to enjoy their weekend.

When Violet and her mom walked outside, Violet saw Isabella waiting to discuss Skye with her. Violet didn't know how she was going to explain this one, but she was going to give it a try. She promised herself that no matter how uncomfortable the conversation became she was going to stick with it. Violet told her mom that she would meet her at the car because she had to talk with Isabella quickly. Violet's conversation was going to be more helpful to Isabella than Isabella had imagined.

"Be honest with me. How do you know about Skye? Did my dad say something to you?" asked Isabella.

Violet didn't know how she was going to break this to her. She couldn't tell her about the shoebox and how her father took her to heaven, where she ran into Skye. Then she thought about how Skye had told her that she visited Isabella in her dreams from time to time, so she was going to stick with that.

"I had a dream that my father took me to heaven, and we were walking in a field where children were playing. A girl then came up to me and told me that she used to be your best friend."

"What else did she say?"

"She wanted me to tell you that she says thank you and that you saved her because you brought her to God."

Isabella was so relieved by Violet's words. Back when she was at the children's hospital with Skye, she was at her bedside along with her family when Skye took her final breath. As she took her final breath, it looked like Skye was trying to get a few last words out, to say something to Isabella, but sadly she wasn't able to. For the longest time, Isabella had been praying to God that Skye was okay and asking God what Skye had intended to say to her. Today Violet had provided that closure for Isabella.

"Violet, you have helped answer my prayers. I always knew there was a reason God made us friends."

"I'm starting to think the same thing as well."

"So are you coming to church on Sunday?"

"Honestly, I'm still thinking about it."

"Oh, okay. Hope to see you there this Sunday. Have a good weekend."

It had been a long four days for Violet, but she had learned so much. The true purpose of the shoebox had been fulfilled. She had been on the journey of a lifetime with her father, and it was through these experiences that her father had been able to teach her some valuable life lessons. These were life lessons that he would've taught her now if he had still been alive. She was able to apply them to her life and improve it. Violet also had a loving support group that helped her along the way. The plan that God had put into motion was almost complete, but there was still one thing left for Violet to do.

Twelve

Sunday morning had come, and the Evans family was at Christ Community Church getting things ready for service. Today's service wasn't an ordinary one. Today was Baptism Sunday, a special day for those who were going to declare their faith, invite the Holy Spirit into their lives, and leave all their burdens behind. Today was also a very special day for Isabella. She was going to give her testimony in front of the entire church and was going to be baptized. Isabella was hoping that Violet would show up because she wanted Violet to hear her story of God's work in her own life firsthand. She was hoping that it would really move Violet and encourage her to move forward in her faith.

"Hey, Dad, do you think she'll show up?" asked Isabella.

"I was thinking the same thing, but something tells me she will," replied Pastor Luke.

"I'm really worried that she won't. Today's message could be really good for her," said Isabella

"I know it will, but you have to remember that everything doesn't happen in your timing. Just because you want her to come to church doesn't mean that she's ready," replied Pastor Luke.

"You're right, Dad. It will all happen in God's timing," said Isabella.

Isabella left her dad and went to find a quiet place to pray. She really did want Violet to experience hearing about the goodness of God. Isabella wanted Violet to hear how she had lived in it and the positive impact it had on her life. This could be the message that Violet needed to hear in order to take her final steps toward God. Isabella didn't only want Violet to hear about the goodness of God; she also wanted her to *experience* it. She prayed, "God, please guide Violet through those doors this morning. Please put it on her heart and her mom's heart to be here at today's service. In your great name I pray, amen."

"Violet, are you ready to go?" asked Violet's mom.

"Just a second, Mom. I need a minute."

Violet stood in front of her mirror anxiously going back and forth about whether she was ready for this. She didn't know what to expect if she did go to church. All this talk about how God would provide the ultimate peace in her life even if she wasn't looking for it seemed unreal to her. The dream, though, was God calling her to step out in faith and find that peace in him.

What if I go and don't feel anything? What if this ends up being for nothing? Violet started to become unsure as to whether she wanted to go to church today, so she went downstairs to talk with her mom.

"Mom, I don't know if I'm ready to go."

"What do you mean? You seem ready. All you have to do is get your shoes on."

"No, Mom, I don't think I'm quite there yet to actually go to church."

Violet's mom knew exactly what Violet was talking about now, but she knew exactly what to say to Violet to encourage her to change her mind.

"Violet, I felt the same way as you do when your dad died, but after a while I realized that it was the right place to be. You will relate to the messages you hear and can apply them to your life."

Isabella stood with her mom at the front door of the church to greet those walking in. She kept hoping she would eventually see Violet and her mom walk up, but she didn't see her. Service was about to start, so Isabella and her mom had to go find their usual front row seats. Isabella asked her mom if they could wait a couple more minutes, but her mom said that today was an important day, and they needed to be on time. Once Isabella and her family took their seats, she kept looking back at the doors to see if Violet and her mom had walked in, but still nothing. The opening song started, and everyone was asked to stand, but Isabella didn't want to. She sat there with her head down. Her mom tapped her on the shoulder and pointed to the right: There were Violet and her mom.

"You have room for two more?" asked Violet.

Without hesitation, the Evans family made room for Violet and her mom. They were really happy that they could join them on this fine Sunday morning.

"Glad you decided to come," Isabella said to Violet.

"Same here," replied Violet.

During the opening song, "Goodness of God," Violet looked around and could tell that there was something different about everyone in the church. People had their arms up in the air, some were on their knees, and others had one arm up and the other over their hearts. The people in the church just looked so at peace, and Violet could feel that vibe in the room. It was as if all their problems had gone away at that very moment. Everyone in the room looked like they didn't have a care in the world.

These people look so joyful, just like the ones that were in the place that my daddy took me to.

The opening song was done, and Pastor Luke told everyone that they had about three minutes before he was going to give his message, so he wanted everyone to go around and greet one another. He made a special note that the congregation should make newcomers feel welcome. Violet didn't really know what to do, so Isabella took her and her mom around to meet all the parishioners. Violet was soon overwhelmed by the friendliness and love everyone displayed. Everyone she was introduced to seemed so friendly and accepting. A lot of the kids at Violet's school were nice, but this was really different. Once the three-minute period was over, everyone returned to their seats and waited for Pastor Luke to go in front of the church to deliver his Sunday sermon.

"Good morning, church. Hope everyone is doing well this morning," said Pastor Luke.

"Good morning, Pastor Luke," responded the congregation in unison.

"Today is a very special day for some of you, for newcomers in particular. Today is Baptism Sunday, which is a declaration of your faith as you witness your fellow parishioner baptized with the Holy Spirit."

"Amen!" responded the congregation, clapping.

"Before we start the baptisms, I am going to give a sermon on the importance of welcoming the Holy Spirit into your life and how it all starts with baptism. Then my daughter, Isabella, will be sharing her testimony with all of you."

Pastor Luke told the story of a man named Horatio Spafford. Horatio Spafford was a successful attorney and real estate investor in the 1860s and a family man. He had a wife, two daughters, and a son. He and his wife Anna were well known for their friendship with the famous preacher D. L. Moody. Life seemed to be going well for him until tragedy struck in the 1870s and continued to strike. The Spafford's' only son came down with scarlet fever and eventually died at the age of four. Then a year later, the Great Chicago fire destroyed every single one of their real estate investments on the shore of Lake Michigan. Horatio was well aware of the toll these disasters had taken on his family and decided to take the family on a holiday in 1873 both for rest and to help Moody with one of the evangelistic campaigns.

Just before they set sail to cross the Atlantic Ocean, a last-minute business development forced Horatio to postpone. He didn't want to ruin the family trip, so he persuaded his wife to take their kids and go ahead without him. Horatio told his wife that he would eventually meet up with them. About nine days later, Horatio got a letter from his wife that read "saved alone." It turned out that the ship Horatio's wife and kids had been on had sunk. His wife, Anna, tried to save their daughters, but they got swept away by the force of the waters. Anna was saved miraculously by a plank that floated underneath her unconscious body and propped her up. Upon hearing the terrible news, Horatio boarded the next ship out to join his mourning wife.

During his voyage, while passing over the place where his family's ship had gone down, Horatio penned the lyrics of the hymn "It Is Well with My Soul." Horatio had been through so much over the previous three years. First, he had lost his son, then his investments, and finally his daughters, but Horatio found this supernatural peace through it all. That was what the hymn was about. It explained that in times of trouble and uncertainty you could only find peace in one place—with the Holy Spirit. Pastor Luke explained that one lyric in particular resonated with him: "Whatever my lot, thou has taught me to say; it is well with my soul." In other words, Horatio had felt he could survive anything with the help of the Holy Spirt.

"See, church, we can always find peace in our situations through the Holy Spirit, and that's what baptism does for us. We're washing away our past burdens and giving them to God. We then go forward, renewed with the Holy Spirit. We're at peace with ourselves because we are now walking with God," said Pastor Luke.

"Amen," said one parishioner.

"Preach!" said another.

"It's also a declaration of our faith that, from this day forward, we have decided to follow God and trust in him wholeheartedly for the rest of our days here on earth," concluded Pastor Luke.

It was now time for Isabella to give her testimony. She began by explaining that she had been brought up in a nice, loving Christian household: her dad a pastor, her mom a devoted wife and loving mother. Isabella had a life that some could only imagine, but not everything was perfect. When Isabella was seven years old, she was diagnosed with terminal cancer. At the age of seven, one can't even comprehend the idea of death, and Isabella was absolutely terrified. The doctors had told her and her parents that she only had a short time to live. Isabella's parents were in disbelief but put their faith in God.

It wasn't that easy for Isabella. She couldn't understand it—if God had this great plan for her, then why was she on the verge of death? Then one day she met a girl named Skye at the children's hospital. Skye was seven as well and had also been diagnosed with terminal cancer. After talking with Skye a couple of times, Isabella learned that Skye was really angry with God about her circumstances and felt the same way as Isabella did. Isabella had a feeling that this was God showing her his plan, which focused on Skye coming to know him. Isabella and Skye met at the kids' café and bonded over their love of ice cream. Their bond grew into the closest of friendships rather quickly.

Isabella continued to go to church every Sunday with her parents, and her father's messages restored Isabella's faith, which made her able to try and help Skye with hers. Talking with Skye about God was really hard at first. Skye didn't have much to say, but Isabella never gave up and kept pouring faith into her day after day and night after night. One day, she saw Skye and her parents hugging each other, and it looked like they were in distress. Skye and her parents had found out that Skye only had about a month left to live.

One night, Skye came into Isabella's room and started asking her about God. Isabella shared the messages she had heard at church every Sunday, and Skye became more open to knowing God. This continued every night. They read the Children's Bible together, and Isabella explained everything from the love of God to finding peace within ourselves by knowing him more. It was the last week of Skye's life, and she wanted to go to church with Isabella and her family. Pastor Luke gave a sermon about the fact that it was never too late to come to God, even on your deathbed. That day Skye gave her life to God, and the very next day she took her last breath surrounded by her loved ones.

Isabella was down on her luck again. Not only did she only have so long to live, but she didn't know if Skye had truly accepted God in her life. She began again to question God and his plan for her. Isabella and her parents eventually got the same news as Skye's family had received: Isabella didn't have long to live. So they brought her to church and had the whole congregation pray over her and not even a week later, she was cancer-free and could go back home.

"Even after that I still questioned God and his plan. Why have me live and not Skye? A couple days ago, a new friend that I made told me that she had a dream about Skye in which Skye told her she had accepted God before she died and is now in heaven. This new friend was having trouble accepting God in her life, too, so now it makes sense that God kept me alive. It was to impact her life the way I impacted Skye's. At least I really hope that I did. I'm done questioning God. I want to seek him only to understand," Isabella concluded her testimony.

The entire congregation stood up and applauded her. Violet was speechless. The stories to her were extremely touching and inspirational. First, a husband and wife had lost everything but found peace within the Holy Spirit and continued to walk with God. The most touching one of all was Isabella's. Isabella was about to lose her life but continued to find peace within God and even had the strength to share her faith with Skye. Even after Skye died, Isabella never walked away from God and kept praying to him. God had her live in order to bring her and Violet together, just as he had brought Isabella and Skye together. Violet, at that moment, saw what her dream had meant and what God had meant by "it's time." It was time for Violet to take a leap into the light and find the freedom that God had waiting for her. To leave all her burdens behind and walk in the presence of the Holy Spirit so she could find peace in her situation and persevere through uncertainty—just like Horatio and Isabella.

Pastor Luke then called up all those who were to be baptized, and one by one, they, too, gave their testimonies and gave their lives to God. Isabella was three people away from the baptism area, and she looked back at Violet. It looked like Violet was in deep thought again. Isabella had a feeling about what Violet was thinking and was hoping she was right. Isabella turned around and waited patiently to get baptized, and then she felt a pull on her arm. It was Violet; she, too, wanted to be baptized today.

"Please be by my side when I do this," said Violet.

"Don't worry, we can go at the same time," Isabella was so emotional at that moment because she had helped touch another person's life by her faith.

It was Violet and Isabella's turn to go, but Violet took the mic and addressed the church first with her testimony.

"Hello, my name's Violet Cooper, and it's my first time back to church in a while. For the longest time I was angry at God for the death of my father. I didn't want to believe anymore and eventually walked away from God. One mention of him and I instantly became angry. These past five days have changed my life. Many individuals who have a special place in my heart helped me get to where I am today. Up until now, though, I still felt empty, and my heart was still in pain. I've come to realize that the only thing that will restore my emptiness is giving my life to God today."

After Violet gave her testimony, Pastor Luke told her to lean back into his arms and plug her nose. He asked her if she was ready to leave everything behind, burdens and all, and she said yes. Then Pastor Luke dunked her under the water. While Violet was underwater, she saw the same light that had been in her dream, and a hand reached out to her through the light. This time Violet grabbed it and came up from under the water. Violet felt that same peace from the light that had been in her dream. For the first time ever, Violet was in the presence of the Holy Spirit.

I never want to leave. I feel. . .whole again, thought Violet. Isabella had been baptized with her, and when they were done, they hugged each other in pure happiness.

The church service was now over. Violet and her mom walked out with Isabella and her family to talk with some of the other parishioners. Everyone came up to Isabella and Violet to congratulate them and commend their bravery in telling their stories of coming to God. As Violet was listening to Isabella talk, she looked up past the crowd of people in the parking lot and saw a man standing there. She left the group to get a better look: it was her dad. He placed his hands in the shape of a heart over his chest, and Violet did the same thing back. They mouthed the words "I love you" to each other. A group of people walked in front of him, and when the group cleared, he was gone.

I'll never forget you, Dad, thought Violet as she walked back to join the group.

"Violet, what was over there?" asked Isabella.

"Oh, just someone who will always hold a special place in my heart," replied Violet.

—⚊—

Later that night, Violet prayed for the first time.

"God, I don't know what tomorrow, the next day or even after that is going to bring me, but I pray that I'll trust you to provide me with something great—greater than I could ever imagine."

Violet's four-year journey may have been over, but her real journey, her journey with God, was about to begin.

Made in the USA
Middletown, DE
31 October 2020

23085480R00106